TEMPER HOUSE

An Emmie Rose Haunted Mystery Book 5

DEAN RASMUSSEN

DARK VENTURE
PRESS

Temper House: An Emmie Rose Haunted Mystery Book 5

Dean Rasmussen

For more information about this book, visit:

www.deanrasmussen.com
dean@deanrasmussen.com

Temper House: An Emmie Rose Haunted Mystery Book 5

Published by: Dark Venture Press

Cover Art: Mibl Art

Developmental & Line Editor: C.B. Moore

❀ Created with Vellum

D r. Alfred Albright tensed in his office chair and held his breath, focusing on the noises coming from the living room. At his age, he had long conquered his fear of the unknown, but there were plenty of dangers in his life to justify his shaking hands and racing heart.

An intruder?

"Who's there?" he called out.

No answer.

What were the odds that anyone could have broken into his house undetected? Slim, but not impossible. He had locked and bolted all the doors—he always made sure of that before settling in for the evening—and he had even put bars on the windows. His condo was at street level, facing an alley, and he had learned to tune out the sounds of the life around his property, as when the homeless passed through in the early morning and scoured the dumpsters. There was always *some* disturbance to distract him from his work, but the noises this evening weren't coming from outside.

Nobody had come through the door or the window. No need for that, of course. Those with knowledge like his own could get around such simple roadblocks if they had studied the right tools.

An intruder of another kind? Yes, but unlike what he'd sensed days ago during his meditation with the obsidian mirror, he could feel its presence clearly now. An intruder of the sort that could get around even his own psychic roadblocks and defenses.

He glanced at the computer he had only just turned off, and at the paperwork scattered across his desk. At least he had time to gather the papers together before stuffing them into a beige folder, pausing for a moment to write across the front with a black marker: Carey Kali.

The hairs along the back of his neck bristled. Someone was watching him. With as much stealth as he could manage, he reached over to the computer and switched it on again.

Why hadn't he gotten the information out to the Carey Kali earlier? He clenched his teeth while straightening his glasses. Too many hours spent reading, researching, and verifying. His drive to get all the details straight in his mind and make the best case to his peers had put him behind schedule. At least Howard would know what to do with his discovery, and the others, if only they received the documents. He hadn't expected an intrusion so soon, and now he was out of time.

A serious miscalculation.

Still, there might still be time to send the documents over email if he acted quickly.

Instead of turning on, however, the computer gave something like a short screech as the internal fan whirred to life, and a flash of light struck the black metal casing. A flame engulfed it before a stream of smoke erupted through the ventilation holes along the side.

Backing away from his desk, he spoke forcefully. "I know you're here."

The lack of a response meant nothing.

The computer was dead, and a toxic smell of burning wires

and plastic filled the air. No sense in trying to put out the fire—it wasn't a flame that would die easily. Now only the papers in his hand held the whole truth. But how could he keep them safe without more time?

He stood with the help of a cane, hugging the folder, and made his way out to the living room. His knees wobbled painfully, finding as much difficulty to support his weak frame as his bony arms. He scanned the area for any signs of the intruder.

It would be brave to head for the front door. Or foolish. He tried anyway, raging against an aging body that had declined rapidly after the death of his wife only a few years earlier. Hurrying as fast as he could, he only made it as far as his recliner before another flash seemed to grab him and throw him back into it.

No sense in trying to run at this point. His phone was out of reach, in his bedroom where he tended to leave it when he was working to avoid distractions. And there was no point in trying to call for help, anyway. The phone would burst into flames, just like his computer had, before he even dialed the first number.

It was watching him now. He could feel its cold, calculating gaze.

The work was finished, but he suspected no one would find it. If he had finished even an hour earlier... He had wanted to explain everything to his Carey Kali friends in person: an old threat they believed to be contained had returned. They would face a determined and daring foe. One that hated him most of all.

For a second he thought of the old days and the lectures in the Great Hall, the charter gatherings around the country and the world. All those bright, passionate minds and spirits longing for the truth and keeping the worst dangers at bay. In recent years, younger members had questioned his precautions. They had questioned the need to contain what they called "natural inquisitiveness." He had gathered information to show them what this inquisitiveness could do when it turned into ambition and a lust for power.

He was eighty-seven years old, the last of his own generation. Yet the charter members taking his place should have learned the lesson by now—listened to the words of a man who had gained so much wisdom—that those willing to play with fire didn't simply stop on their own. But time passed, and people forgot.

And playing with fire was no exaggeration, in this case. A warmth filled the room as the smoke from his computer drifted higher. The intruder was coming for him.

The presence stirred across the living room. Something unseen stood watching. The extractor had caught up with him.

"You can't win," he said aloud. "They'll find you. They'll root you out."

Again, no answer.

If only the cloudy vision he'd seen within the obsidian mirror had revealed the full truth earlier. His premonitions were rarely inaccurate, but this intrusion had come out of nowhere. The mirror's darkness had come alive to suggest that something was foul, but a greater darkness had obscured the true depth of the abyss. Not even a lifetime of confronting shadows and devils had prepared him for this moment.

But one thing he'd learned was that nothing was set in stone. The future existed as a stream of shifting probabilities, and the will of one spirit could set the darkest visions ablaze with a single spark or extinguish the same with a single breath.

He wasn't so concerned about himself. He only wished he could have done more to avoid what he knew would happen to everyone else. The dark vision had jarred him into action, but he had miscalculated how quickly things would escalate.

The irony of the moment struck him. He had always prodded his students to stay on top of things, to always be prepared and never let their guard down. He'd failed at his own lesson.

Glancing at the folder again, he stared at the name Carey Kali.

They couldn't help him now.

A spark appeared in the air several feet away. He stared at the intruder's appearance, amazed that it had twisted such a beautiful gift into such an abomination. Of course, only a piercing light such as this could have bypassed his own psychic protections. This whole time, they had been developing this knowledge. Dark, forbidden knowledge.

The light hovered and expanded vertically to form the ghostly shape of a genderless figure. Its silhouette wavered and faded into the background like a sun peeking through the clouds.

He squinted to make out the details. He suspected their name but wanted to make sure. Maybe there was still time to scribble down the specter's identity—except that it wasn't really going to let him leave his recliner. His heart ached, quite literally, after so many battles.

"Be quick about it," he ordered. He had showed the same mercy against his enemies and perhaps deserved this last courtesy.

Before he could take another breath, a ray of light blasted forward into his chest like a spear slicing through his heart. His mind flooded with pain as a white flame seemed to emanate from every pore of his skin. An inferno engulfed him, starting with his chest and spreading through his flesh until his lungs and heart collapsed and burned within the searing blaze.

Even as he lost consciousness forever, he saw his own spirit flash out of his body and hover in the air for a moment, and then a black void swallowed him.

2

"Hello, Sarah."

"Good morning, Alex."

Sarah closed her eyes and cleared her mind. His voice was so clear—no electronics, no static, no tricks. Pure telepathy.

"Alone again?" he asked.

"I have the day off. Emmie and Jason just left for a vacation in New Orleans. I'm not complaining. It's nice to get some quiet time alone and get caught up on some sleep... er, I mean, studying my craft."

"I understand. The Lady of Light deserves a break," he said with a flare of humor.

"I certainly do." She laughed.

For the first time since meeting Emmie, Sarah felt empowered by a vibrant presence she could relate to. Not a lost spirit begging for her help, but rather the bright spirit of another empath offering his help.

She had communicated with him every day for a few days now, but the time had been exciting. As when receiving a phone call from a pen pal in a faraway land, she had listened with curiosity and cautiousness, and had sensed his genuine interest

6

in her abilities and joy that he had found someone like himself in the world.

His name was Alex Temper, a name that had held no significance to her until she had done some research on him, connecting him with a family on the east coast of Florida. She had checked him out—thoroughly—but had kept it all to herself for some strange reason. Was she afraid that Emmie or Jason would condemn her for talking with a stranger? It wasn't like she was a wide-eyed child being lured into a van with the promise of candy. Making connections with other psychics was to be expected. Networking, but on a higher level.

His telepathic presence had arrived at all hours of the day, sometimes when she was alone and sometimes with Emmie, but her friend hadn't seemed to notice. It was like a message coming on a frequency only she could receive. It baffled Sarah at first how they could communicate over such long distances, and how he had found her from across the country, which almost seemed miraculous without the aid of any technology. But his fellowship was insightful, meaningful and empowering.

"Your light," he had explained after first contacting her, "is like a beacon in the night, so I just followed it back to you. It wasn't so difficult, if you know what to look for."

"So you *were* looking?"

"I'm always looking for another spirit like me. Human nature, I guess. It's wonderful just to know someone else is out there with the same gift."

He had found her only a few days after she'd returned home from Whisper House and had complimented her on her stunningly brilliant aura that had easily caught his spiritual eyes from such a great distance. He wanted to know everything about her, speaking directly into her mind in a calm, soothing voice. So many questions at first.

"When did you discover your gift?" he'd asked.

"When I was quite young, and my grandmother pointed out to me that I was different."

"How have you used it since you discovered it?"

"I suppressed it in my teen years, then after I met Emmie, I could finally express my true self. Thank God for her or I'm not sure where I'd be right now."

"How did you survive the hurricane of emotions an empath endures during childhood and adolescence?"

"I survived," was all she'd said.

And the questions flowed, back and forth, as they shared their experiences like two children discovering they were long-lost twins.

They exchanged little personal information, concentrating mostly on her experiences as an empath. That's all he wanted, it seemed. To hear about her struggles and failures and successes. In a way, it was more intimate than a face-to-face conversation, although not uncomfortable. Safe.

She could feel his presence so strongly now as she sat on the edge of her bed and allowed the warmth of his thoughts to fill her mind.

Alex continued, "After you're done napping—oh, I mean *studying*—do you have any other big plans?"

"Not really. It's too cold for a walk."

"What a shame. You should really do something fun, something interesting." Alex went silent for a moment. "Listen, I don't want to seem forward, but I just arrived here in Minneapolis, just stepped off the plane. I'm speaking this morning at a business convention, and I'm wondering if you'd like to meet in person. Just for coffee to talk, that sort of thing. Very informal."

Sarah's breath stopped for a moment. She could still sense his warmth within his energy, even from that distance. But Finn... "I'm not sure." She laughed uncomfortably. "Is this turning into some weird kind of Tinder?"

He laughed. "I'm sorry. No. Please don't misunderstand me. Nothing like that. I'm a recent widower, as I think I mentioned before. And you've made it very clear your heart belongs to a guy named Finn. Is that right?"

"Yes, that's right."

"Lucky man. But I thought it might be nice to finally see each other, and exchange an old-fashioned face-to-face conversation for a change. Would you be up for that this afternoon?"

She glanced across her room at the framed photos on the back of her dresser. Moments of her time spent with Emmie or Finn captured on camera, and now even a new photo with Jason. There *was* room for another friend.

"Sure," she answered finally.

"Wonderful. I'll text you the address."

"I look forward to it."

The communication faded like someone's voice fading as they walked away. She sat in silence for a moment, then glanced over at a photo on her dresser. One of her favorites. It showed Finn embracing her shortly after they'd first met. Had Emmie captured the exact moment he'd won her heart?

Her phone dinged from the dresser and startled her back to reality. A surge of excitement swept through her as she jumped toward it and checked the name on the incoming message. Had Finn read her mind and sent her a message?

No, it was just Emmie sharing a quick video of the view from their hotel room. Nothing that resembled the French Quarter from what Sarah could see, but the streets of New Orleans bustled as a horse-drawn carriage split traffic, passing below their window.

A quick check of her other messages revealed what she'd assumed. No new messages from Finn. Seven days now of silence. He had stuck a knife in her heart when he left, and now the blade made another twist.

She typed out a quick message to him but hesitated to send it. If he had left and wanted privacy, why bother?

Deleting it, she pushed aside her phone and stood up. At

least she would have a good reason to change out of her pajamas on her day off. She rushed to prepare for her meeting with Alex.

3

"At least it's not snowing," Emmie said as she hurried along the downtown New Orleans sidewalks beside Jason.

"Bad luck to say that out loud." Jason pointed to the gray sky. "Don't tempt the gods. Only a few degrees colder and it might."

Christmas displays lined the dated storefronts and streets. Every pedestrian was either bundled up or cowering in the driving December wind around them. As they passed a few historic buildings, the arched doorways and hanging foliage along the balconies reminded her of Mardi Gras. She could even hear the jazz music and nightlife echoing in her mind.

Jason gripped her hand firmly but softly, staying by her side as they moved through the crowd. "It occasionally snows here, from what I hear."

She shook her head. "Then I can't really consider this a vacation. Only beaches and sunshine if I'm expected to really unwind."

"It's just business this time. And haven't you just had a beach vacation?"

"You mean the vacation that I don't even remember after everything that happened at Whisper House?" She peered at him. "Do we at least have time to stop at the French Quarter? To warm up?"

He pulled her closer. "I'm sure we can make time for that."

A storefront across the street was full of oddities similar to what she had found at Betty's: hanging voodoo dolls, statues and figurines, and dream catchers. A row of candles beneath the store's name seemed to beckon the curious.

Emmie gestured at it with a smirk. "Maybe a chance to get Finn some Christmas presents?"

"Oh yes. Finn would just love something like that, I'll bet, after Hyde House."

"Then let's go!" She made a move to cross the street.

Jason tugged her back and steered her in a different direction. "Talk about wasting your money. I'm taking you to a real place, you know. Where you'll find real..." He gestured back toward the store. "... this-sort-of-thing."

"Why do I suspect I won't be able to afford anything *real?*"

They made a sharp left turn toward their destination, and she giggled as he stopped suddenly within a brown, weathered doorway, looked around and kissed her. Much as she liked to tease him about not taking her to the sun and sea, the truth was she was very happy right there. When he pulled away, his dark eyes crinkling at the corner and looking mischievous, she just felt lucky, that was all. She couldn't help seeing the irony behind finding someone when she had been jealous of Sarah and Finn— and brushed away the flash of Finn, half frozen, running after her on the ice; they had gone their different ways for the moment, and she could not deny that she felt some relief at being here just with Jason.

"Joker," she pushed him away. He shouldn't know how much she liked him, or he'd get a big head.

"Bully," he said and pulled her to the door.

It looked so... unremarkable.

Emmie paused. "We're going in *here?* Is it a shop? Are they even open?"

He winked at her. "Not without an appointment." He rang the buzzer and not long after the camera in it became green, and the door clicked.

Leading her inside, Jason closed the door behind them, shutting out the chilly wind Emmie thought would never let up.

Stillness and a brightly lit old staircase greeted them. No signs of a formal business. An antique chandelier lit an oriental rug that covered the wooden stairs up one flight.

"So..." Emmie said, "what kind of store is this?"

Jason extended his elbow toward her. "Specialty items for people like us."

She grabbed on. "Like your customers, you mean."

"The man you're about to meet lets me know when he has something or things that might interest me," he said as they climbed the steps. "I like to think he calls me first, but maybe that's too naïve. Second or third?"

She scoffed. "You must really hate that."

"I'm not Finn, you know. I'm a realist."

On the second floor, they followed a short hallway around to a single door on their right. The door opened before they arrived and a thin elderly man with thick white hair stepped out. A broad grin was fixed on his face. Adjusting his square glasses, he watched them approach. He wore expensive jeans and a black turtleneck that accentuated his slight frame. The lights reflected off his highly polished shoes, and he straightened as they approached, as if proud to flaunt his wealth.

"Jason," he said with the same tight smile.

The men shook hands at the door.

"Hello, Roger. You texted, and I came running. As always."

The man's smile—or grimace?—now conveyed shock. "Haven't you heard the news?"

Jason glanced at Emmie. "What news?"

Roger silently led them inside. Scattered antique rugs, apparently rarer than the one over the stairway, covered the marble inlay floors. The front room was more like a showroom in a museum than anything you might see in someone's home. Two finely crafted oak bookcases served as a curio display gallery, each shelf showcasing a handful of carefully placed oddities lit from above.

Emmie recognized a few of the items as antique medallions and jewelry, although some of them looked out of place in such a quietly lavish environment. Things like a collection of small, flat circular stones and a circle of twisted gold wire caught her attention.

As Roger motioned them in and walked before them, she walked closer to the stones and read the small plaque beside it. "Norse Runestones: Södermanland, Sweden, 1079 A.D." Why did she have the impression that was the least important stuff he would have? His "trade" items, she was sure, would be way more exclusive and not displayed except to serious buyers like Jason.

After his question, Roger had stepped over to a small wet bar set into the wall and now poured a glass of whiskey from a crystal decanter. His hands trembled as he sipped the drink and turned back to them. "I'm so sorry. Where are my manners? Would you like a drink?"

"Depends on what the news is," Jason answered, frowning at the man.

Emmie studied Roger's expression—the look of someone who might have seen a ghost.

Roger gazed down at his drink. "I never thought it would happen here."

"What happened?" Jason insisted slowly.

The man lifted his phone off the counter and unlocked his screen while tilting it toward them to reveal a news article. "Can you believe that?" He laughed nervously.

Emmie and Jason read the headline he was showing them: "Elderly professor found burned inside New Orleans condo." The article, dated that same day, talked about a man found so burned that the police compared the manner of his death to an attempted cremation. It wasn't the gruesome manner of the victim's death that jumped out at Emmie, however, but the victim's name.

Dr. Albert Albright. The man who'd attempted to train her and Jason to "live up to their full psychic potential" as children by tossing them into the deep end of the spirit-world pool. The trauma of his methods still lingered in her nightmares.

Emmie met Jason's gaze. "That can't be..."

Jason's eyes were as wide as hers. "He *does* live somewhere in New Orleans."

"No way."

"You knew Dr. Albright?" Roger asked. He nodded briefly. "Of course. Figures. It's a small world, if you think of it."

"It can't be him," Emmie said. But in her heart, she knew it was true.

"It's—" Roger looked at Jason meaningfully. "Not natural."

Both Jason and Emmie continued reading the article's brief paragraphs. The police suggested the hypothesis that this was a revenge crime by someone connected with the occult, having found a treasure trove of psychic and magic material in the professor's home. And the neighbors who were usually inter-viewed under such circumstances spoke of Albright as a quiet, studious man—a retired history professor.

The couple stepped away from the counter as Roger poured himself more whiskey. The old man's hands still trembled with every sip.

Jason told Emmie in a low voice, "We should talk outside."

Roger now leaned against the corner of the bar as if to steady himself and looked at Jason. "What does it mean? What kind of thing is it?"

"I have no idea," Jason said. "But we'll leave business for another day, if you don't mind."

Their host nodded slowly, then rushed forward. "You'll tell me, won't you?" he asked, holding Jason by the shoulder. "If something is on the loose."

"If I find out anything, and it's something you need to worry about," Jason said. "Sure." As Roger didn't let go, Jason said, "I promise."

When they managed to get outside and Jason had pulled the door shut behind them, as if keeping the nervous Roger inside, his phone pinged. He took it out and angled it toward Emmie. Even as they read one message, another popped up. All of them talked about one subject: Dr. Albert Albright.

"Looks like everyone learned the same way and at the same time," Jason mumbled as he typed a message quickly. "I'm contacting someone close to him."

One of the messages he'd received claimed Dr. Albright's death was a surreal piece of vengeance, just as the news had suggested. As they moved along, he received an answer: Albright's furniture and apartment were intact, with no signs of fire damage or an intrusion. The only other items that had been destroyed in the flames were his computer and papers around his chair.

"I didn't know so many people knew Dr. Albright," Emmie said.

"A family member got into his place and... word traveled fast, considering the circumstances."

Emmie threw him a curious look. Jason certainly knew a lot of people from a psychic world she had avoided after her dealings with the doctor. "Definitely murder, isn't it? And definitely not a *normal* murder. How could only *he* have burned and nothing around him? Could they have taken him somewhere and—"

He only looked at her over his brow, shook his head slowly and mumbled, "You've come across spontaneous combustion in psychic phenomena? Or... the combusting of another?" He took a deep breath. "This could mean we are in for strange times."

"We?" she asked. "I don't—" She wanted to say that she didn't belong to those organizations or schools or whatever they were, but she no longer knew whether that was true. Jason had found her—had known about her even from across the country. Others probably did too.

They didn't say another word until the street door was shut behind them and they left the building. The drone of passing cars masked their conversation.

"Do you know where Albright lived?" Emmie asked, while trying to cover her face from the wind.

Jason stopped and turned to her. "Are you serious? I was just thinking maybe we should get the hell out of New Orleans."

"And I was just thinking," she said, holding on to his arm again, "that if this is something significant, it's in our interest to know. We're involved in this, whether we want to be or not."

"In a very *distant* way," he said.

"Not so distant. My parents and Betty were involved in the same whatever-it-is that Albright belonged to."

"Carey Kali," Jason said.

"They have a name?" She made a face at him. "How come I didn't come across it?"

"They don't write it down anywhere. I mean, maybe they do, but not in any books you might have read from Betty."

Emmie considered Jason's words as they continued walking. There were still so many things she didn't know about the psychic world. Maybe her parents had left her more information about their involvement in all this—something still to be found hidden in a book, in a bank vault, a sealed envelope somewhere. Facing the harsh reality of the psychic world with a void of knowledge was far from ideal, but at least Jason was there to fill in the gaps.

"Yeah," she went on impulsively, as if they hadn't stopped discussing it, "we can't keep jumping in and out all the time."

"What are you talking about?"

"We need to go there."

"What would going to his house do, apart from calling attention to us? The police will have cleared the scene by now. But I'm not sure anyone would let us inside. The way he died will generate a lot of sensational news, conspiracy theories, that sort of thing. Besides, I thought you hated this guy."

"Not *hated*, so much. I definitely had issues with his methods, but we can't just walk away from this. Despite all the bad memories, I wouldn't wish a death by burning on anyone. Things keep being connected to my parents."

"*Distantly*," Jason emphasized.

"Even so, I won't just let this grow out of control until we can't do anything about it."

He stopped and faced her this time. "You do know you aren't being paid to investigate this, right?"

She could tell by his expression that he wasn't interested in pursuing it. Leaning into him, she narrowed her eyes and spoke a little louder. "We've got to go there and find his spirit."

"His group is all over this already. They might consider it an obstruction of their investigation if we snooped around there."

"So let's obstruct."

Jason tilted his head and raised his eyebrows. "Oh God. Why am I remembering only now how stubborn you can be?"

"Then you should also remember that it takes a force of nature to change my mind."

"Thought you wanted some rest." Putting his hand in the pockets of his coat, Jason looked at the sky. "I guess it's no different from what I've been pushing you to do for money."

"Exactly. And I'll do this one pro bono."

❧ 4 ❧

Finn had never stepped foot in Cuba before, though he had
always wanted to come and knew he would find a vibrant,
colorful, humid place. And Jason had assured him that he would
get solace and answers here from a woman he knew. A "good
witch" named Natalia, as Jason had said, laughing uncharitably
when Finn backed away in horror.

"I said *good*," Jason had insisted.

Unsure if such a thing existed, Finn had boarded a flight,
arrived in Havana and promptly taken a ramshackle bus—the
only kind he liked—to the coastal town of Santiago.

After dropping off his bag at a seafront hotel that had a
certain mid-century flare, he had hailed a taxi in the shape of an
old Ford sedan from the 1970s painted bright yellow. Despite
Natalia's somewhat subjective texted directions and the driver's
assurance that he knew the area well, they had gotten lost for a
while and finally found the dirt path toward the beach. He had
spotted the three palm trees that "leaned like they were sleeping," as Natalia had written, and the "red and white thingie,"
which turned out to be an umbrella over a fruit stand on the
road, and spotted the "white house, a little dusty, with the blue

shutters and the red top." By which she had meant the tiled roof, as he saw now.

As he got out of the car and pulled his white shirt away from his sweaty back, he could almost feel the ground shaking—but it was the sound of drums, drifting clearly to him as he counted some colorful pesos to give the driver.

"Ooh, you start with the Santería, my gringo," the man said, laughing and pocketing the money. "Good luck with that."

"Well, Fidel was a fan," Finn said as he walked toward the drums and singing.

Turning around the corner of a house to see the beach, he spotted a small crowd of men and women dancing in white ceremonial outfits and offerings placed beside the shore. He had never witnessed one happening spontaneously, so he slowed down and watched them.

The offerings sent a chill up his spine, reminding him of Hyde House. *Good witch, my*— But the faces of the dancers were full of joy, and they were throwing roses into the sea. Hypnotized by their dancing and singing, he barely reacted when a woman's laugh burst through the air.

Finn located the young woman, who was waist-deep inside the seas with white roses in her hand, which she was scattering as she laughed again, looking at him, and called out, "Finn!"— although she sang it, *Fiii-iii-iiinn*—"I know it's you!"

The other worshippers didn't turn around as the young woman swayed her hips past the waves, her white dress clinging to a very pleasant form, and rushed over to him. Her wet black hair stuck to her shoulders as she smiled.

"Jason," Finn said under his breath, "you miserable..."

Because of course this was Natalia, and she was beautiful. And maybe Clever Jason thought that would make Finn forget what had brought him here in the first place. Every step Natalia took in his direction revealed a healthy sensuality that she could not have disguised if she'd wanted. She didn't bother to wait for his response before she threw herself in his arms and hugged him, wet and all.

"Hello!" he cried out with exaggerated glee, holding his hands in the air as if they might accidentally land anywhere on her curves.

"You've arrived just in time," she said, nodding toward the sea.

"Time for what?"

"We are celebrating Yemayá. You know, goddess of the sea?"

There was no trace of an accent in her English, but Jason had said she spent her childhood and teen years in the US, arriving with immigrant parents, and then decided in her early twenties she loved her own country too much to give it up.

She was smiling up at him as she continued, "Waters of life and love, you know? And white roses are for purity."

"Sure."

Now she looked at him more closely. "A pure love that lasts a lifetime."

Yeah, well. Jason was also a bigmouth. But everlasting love was jumping the gun a little, anyway—except that she was obviously teasing him.

"Not in a party mood, I see," she said, and nodded toward the dusty white house. "Let's go home."

Finn wasn't used to feeling embarrassed, and he could tell Natalia was just brimming with life like Yemayá or something, but he did want to slip his hand out of hers as she pulled him over the sand to the house. He finally found the excuse of his shoes, which were filling with sand, and stopped to remove them. He held one in each hand, but she just grabbed his arm and glued herself to it as she kept talking.

Her smell caught him off guard, an intoxicating aroma of sea, roses and something else, sweet but not sugary, that he had never encountered before. Had she put it on for the ceremony? Hopefully not for him.

"Here we are," she said, stopping in front of the house. It had a veranda made of polished concrete with red dye and was full of tracks of sand, as if people visited all the time and rarely used the broom leaning against the wall. A hammock waved and turned in the breeze to their left, and only half of the blue shutters were open. But then the sun and wind were strong, judging by the crooked pieces and bleached exterior of the shutters.

"Gain all hope ye who enter," she pronounced happily, gesturing toward the wide front door.

Didn't Dante say the opposite of the entrance to hell? Was she saying this was paradise?

Natalia seemed to read his mind. "Plenty of wayward souls have passed through here."

"What about the bodies?" he asked, a little nervously.

"They came with!" she cried, opening the door.

"And left with too?"

She gave the big laugh again. As they walked into a darkened and slightly bare interior, exotic aromas calmed his nerves. Strange how that always happened in his travels.

He detected wood, the sweetness of fruit, and burnt leaves. Then a smell he didn't recognize, so he sniffed the air intentionally.

"Agua de violetas," Natalia said, stepping barefoot through the entrance. She wasn't even looking at him, and again could probably tell what he was thinking. She smiled at him over her shoulder. "Violet water. All Cuban children smell of it, and some of us can't quit when we grow up."

The walls of the foyer were bare and in need of a coat of paint, though Natalia didn't seem overly concerned by that as she tracked more sand and dripped water all over the old wooden floors. Just beyond the entryway, in the room to the right, was an area walled off by hanging curtains. Through a crack in the curtain, Finn spotted a man lying on the floor dressed in white, with leaves over his eyes and covered in a mixture of what seemed like herbs and oil as if he were a fish about to go in the oven.

"An ebbo misi," Natalia said, backtracking to Finn's side. "A cleansing bath, except I'm *marinating* him."

Finn couldn't help giving a laugh.

"Bitter herbs," she added. "Rue and rosemary."

He sniffed the air again as they kept walking. "Why bitter?"

"Sometimes people think they need sweet herbs to cleanse disappointment or a hurt," she said. "But it depends. If they harbor a secret desire for vengeance, then they need bitter herbs."

Secret desires... That's what he had harbored. Horrible secret desires. It gave him a pang in his heart, but it also made him shake his head as he imagined himself being covered in sticky stuff and... marinated.

"Might not be your case," Natalia said. "Let's not jump the gun."

He recoiled as she used the same expression he had in his head at the beach. *A coincidence, idiot.* Except she was smiling up at him again as if she knew everything.

"You're psychic, of course," he blurted out.

"Oh, labels," she said, flapping a hand.

She led him through the house to one of the back rooms with walls full of hand-painted banners and colorful symbolic murals that someone had clearly painted with great care. Some of them reminded him of the murals he had seen at Whisper House, and that again sent a surge of anxiety through his chest.

Jason's words came back to him: *You can trust her.*

He spotted some statues on the floor at one end of the room. Orishas, African gods brought over and adapted, and added to. Like Yemayá. They didn't spook him; he had some at home.

After looking around the room, he narrowed his eyes at her and insisted, "You read minds?"

Instead of answering, Natalia leaned forward a little. "You've got beautiful eyes, Finn."

"Uh... Thanks?"

She continued, "But there's a heaviness behind them, something blocking the light from passing through."

Finn looked away. "You can see all that, huh?"

"Not that hard to see." Her smile faded for the first time as a solemn expression took over.

He had the sudden urge to leave. The smells, the flirting, the sense that the *good witch* was messing with his mind—he was done playing with any of that stuff. He was out of his depth, and he wanted his life to be normal—except it was too late for that. No chance to back out now.

"This room is too busy. You're thinking too much, and clinging to what you know," Natalia said. She gestured down a bare hall and to the right. "We can talk in the back. A little more peaceful there, and clear."

He took a deep breath and touched his pocket. "Do you need payment beforehand? I—"

"You pay the orishas, later," she said, waving at the statues as she walked away from him. "They like candy. Rum too."

Sounded like they had a sweet tooth.

Finn followed her down the hall into a room that only had two emerald-green sofas with a small circular table between them.

Large open windows looked out into a backyard full of lush green plants and flowers. He imagined she might grow her own herbs there, *like a good witch.* Trees obscured the neighbors, but a warm, bright sunlight flooded in, and the smell of salt reminded Finn that he was close to the sea. Again, the smells calmed him.

Natalia appeared at his side with a glass. "It's only water."

"I'm not—"

"You need to drink. For purity."

Finn kept himself from scoffing as he took the glass and watched her face while drinking it. Would she drug him?

They took a seat across from each other.

"Look..." Finn leaned forward. "I'm not sure what Jason told you, but there is something bothering me, something big."

"Jason told me about the house. What happened there?"

Finn fell back. "All right..." he said, slightly disconcerted.

She made a looping gesture with her finger. "You've been walking around all worried I might do something to you. Well, I also have to know who comes into my house. Right?"

"Right," he said tightly. True, she had to know before she even accepted seeing him. "So, there you are. I tried to kill two women. With an ax."

Natalia tilted her head at him. "You tried to kill your best friend and the woman you love with an ax."

His eyes fell away from hers. Now, that hurt worse than an ax. "There you go... In a nutshell."

"And what do you think you need, that Jason would send you to me?"

"Kind of hard to tell," Finn said, recovering some of his spirit, "since you won't tell me what you do besides *marinating guys.*"

She grinned as her head went back and let out that delicious laugh again. But then the head came down and tilted the other way and she just waited.

"I need to find out about myself. I need... I *desperately* need to know if I'm psychic or not."

"Is that what you think you need?" she asked softly.

"Please," he said, and all the tension he had battled for weeks seemed to wrap around him like giant tentacles reaching in from the sea. "Please, let's not play with words. With... concepts."

"Someone told you that a spirit could not possess you to do what you did," she said, "unless you were psychic."

He nodded miserably, hoping Jason's introduction of him might save time. Her mouth slightly twisted to one side, as if she didn't quite agree. They were going into concepts after all. "Tell me."

"Your Western thinking," she said. "It's results-oriented. You think in terms of time. You think in terms of achievement." She touched her chest. "I don't deal with that because it isn't wise.

It's no good. It's why I didn't like learning in your country and came back."

Familiar with Eastern and African philosophies, Finn said, "You mean you prefer a philosophy more like slow food."

"*Exactamente,*" she said. "It's slowing down, breathing things in, looking, listening, feeling. The orishas speak to you like your body speaks to you, below the noise of your mind, your intellect. It's wisdom gained over the centuries. You know about yin and yang, right?"

"It's on every yoga mattress."

"Black and white curving into each other and there is black in the white and white in the black. And which is good? And which is bad?"

"You still spoke of purity..."

"Not as you think of it. For me, purity is the state of mind in which you just... know."

"You said the man in there with the herbs harbored revenge—"

"We contain multitudes. All of us. But you guys get scared of that. You overreact."

He raised his eyebrows. "Yeah, getting an ax to kill my friends is a bit of overreaction."

It was her turn to lean forward. "Everything is possible in the realm of thought. It's not as cut and dried as you think it is. Being psychic, not being psychic."

"I need to find—"

"Your truth, Finn?"

Finn cringed and ran his fingers through his hair. "There's that word again. Everything's about truth lately."

"It's a thing, you know." She smiled. "In the psychic world or not."

"I'm just so tired of hearing it. I just need someone to help me remove this horrible"—he gestured over his body—"*truth* inside me. So that I never have to face it again."

"You want the results, but you can't remove thoughts and

feelings like a wart. It's who you are forever. That's something nobody can change."

Finn's heart sank.

She continued, "But the point is, it's all flowing through you all the time. All the emotions. All the thoughts, including of killing who you love."

"*Each man kills the thing he loves...*" he said softly.

"Yes. We're full of poems today. But why do you think poets said these things? Poets are connected to the universe itself and they speak that word you don't want to hear."

"Natalia—"

"Control that impatience. The concept is *your* problem. Someone in your world, where everything is black and white, told you that if you aren't psychic, blah blah blah. And I could bring you some cards or objects and make you close your eyes and guess or some bullshit like that. But *the truth*, Finn..."

Once more, she leaned forward to stare deep into him.

"The truth is, I saw it right away. There is not the slightest hint of psychic ability in you."

꧁ 5 ꧂

S arah spotted Alex immediately: a man in his early thirties with wavy blond hair, worn slightly long, sitting alone in the crowded cafe and staring out of the massive windows that faced a congested Nicollet Avenue as pedestrians scurried by on the sidewalk. A brightly lit Christmas tree rose to the ceiling behind him, and each table was adorned with decorative bows and snowflakes and Santa cutouts. It wasn't Jason's looks that gave him away, but instead his emotional signature. He was exactly as she had envisioned him during their oddly spiritual communication. His face was somehow lonely, but he also held a confidence that was mirrored in his dark gray suit and slate-blue tie.

She walked over to him as her heart beat faster, shaking off the snow that had stuck to her pant legs after inadvertently stepping into a deep patch of snow. The winter air had chilled her skin, but she warmed quickly among the other patrons as she made her way over to him, preparing in her mind what she would say. The smell of coffee added an extra layer of anticipation.

Before she could get to him, he turned suddenly as if sensing her approach, and they met each other's gaze. His change in expression was instant as he stood, his face bright and smiling.

"You made it!" Alex shook her hand, then leaned forward briefly for a casual hug. "It's so wonderful to finally meet you."

"Same here," Sarah said, removing her jacket and hanging it over the back of her chair.

Alex gestured to the busy street. "It amazes me that so many people voluntarily live in freezing weather like this."

Sarah shrugged. "You get used to it... eventually."

"I love the warmth and sunshine too much, but I guess I didn't grow up here so I don't consider it home either. My home is back in Florida with my family."

"Minnesota can get brutally cold, that's for sure, but my friends and family are here. I guess we all make a lot of crazy sacrifices for family." Sarah sat at the table while Alex remained standing and gestured toward the main counter. "Let me get you something. Anything at all."

Sarah nodded once. "Just a coffee with cream for me."

"Nothing to eat? If you're hungry..."

She shook her head. "I'm not."

He met her gaze again for a moment as if he could almost read her mind. Not an uncomfortable moment, but an understanding that this meeting was the start of something special because...

You're just like me.

He turned away, and she watched him as he walked over to the counter and ordered. His interaction with the barista was gentle and pleasant, without any of the overt flare that some men exhibited when trying to impress a woman. Perfect. He wasn't in town just to see her, and he knew this wasn't a date.

He returned a little while later with their coffees and sat across from her. She sipped her coffee slowly after cooling it down, warming her hands against the cup as she held it. The tables around them were empty, but the drone of the conversations and clatter within the café canceled out any chance someone might overhear them, even from a distance.

It didn't take long for them to get comfortable, picking up

their conversation like two friends that had known each other for years. Soon they were talking about their abilities, the thing that made them different from all others surrounding them.

"You found me from such a long distance. I don't even know how that works. Can I find someone? Do the same?"

He studied her for a moment. "Possibly. Do you come from a long line of psychics?"

"Just my grandmother, like I told you. Maybe there were others, but she never told me, and neither did my mom."

"Did she ever visit you? Like I did?"

Sarah thought about it. "Not the same way. I would think I felt her thoughts sometimes. And since she died, I see her in dreams, like she's guiding me."

"Guiding you from beyond death?" he said almost mournfully. His eyes were a strange gray, with very little blue or green in them, and they had deepened.

"I guess... I mean, I know it's not possible..."

"Do you?" Now he looked down at his coffee, and she remembered he had lost a wife and child.

"I mean—we know souls exist. But if they die naturally, they pass. So I don't know exactly what those dreams are."

Alex shrugged. "Even I don't know a lot of things, and my family had a school. We're always finding out stuff."

"True. Emmie's been psychic all her life, and Finn isn't psychic, but he reads as much as he can on the subject—keeps us updated on the latest psychic news whether we like it or not." She smiled. "And I've already learned so much from the recent experiences. The process hasn't been easy, that's for sure. More like they've thrown me into the deep end of the pool. Sink or swim."

"No one knows everything. Not the books, not the experts. Not anyone." He gave her a small smile. "We are all sinking or swimming. Or both."

Sarah broadened her smile. "Emmie had the same experience growing up. I think that's what bonds us, our shared suffering."

"A heart can only suffer so much alone. We need family and friends to survive. But you shouldn't worry because your light will attract all the right spirits."

"This *special light* you keep talking about... It was something very strange and new. It just... happened."

"How so?"

Now she had even more of his attention. He just crossed his arms on the table and leaned forward to hear.

"I can't explain it. There were souls that had been trapped in a house for a very long time. They couldn't accept they were dead. They thought we were. A mother and her child were trapped there, and in pain. And when we went to try to free them, I just felt—I felt a surge, like I was drawing them into me. Not like before, when I used to help them go off. But like they were passing through me."

His face changed, although he didn't seem to move. "What happened then?"

"Emmie said I just became this incredibly bright light. And I mirrored the little boy's brother, and he came through. The mother too. And then all the souls, they all passed through me, and I felt this unbearable... joy."

Her gaze strayed to the shifting gray clouds outside as the memory filled her mind. A family hurried past the window outside, and she followed their faces for a moment, sensing their intense joy and togetherness. She had felt that same expanding oneness with the souls at Whisper House as they had passed through her in the most beautiful way possible. When she looked at Alex again, it seemed to her his face had grown a little pale, though he was already quite fair.

"The door of light..." he mumbled.

"What?"

"Have you never heard of it? The door of light?"

Sarah thought about it and shrugged. "Not really."

Sitting back, he scoffed. "It can't be. It's extremely rare."

"But what is it?" she insisted.

"Literally a door between life and death. So much light that it can draw the spirits like you apparently did—and a lot more."

"Like what?"

"Like use the light in incredible ways." He seemed to study her face and added quickly, "For good, of course. That joy you felt, like the joy of standing at the door of creation."

"That's a way of putting it..." She liked it.

"You can make others feel it. You can... Sarah, you can heal people. Wounded souls."

Her thoughts, faster than she wanted them to be, flew to Finn. The image of his desperately pained eyes staring at the floor in his room as he had tried to understand himself. She'd wanted to do something for him, but no amount of compassion and kindness had gotten through.

He was wounded. Deeply wounded. And worse now. The man before her too. And Emmie, in her special way.

Sarah's own mother, battling the sadness of a divorce and her ex-husband—

My dad.

—with a new woman, feeling she had wasted her life.

And Sarah herself. And just about everyone around them.

"Yes," Alex said gently. "There is a lot of suffering."

"Wouldn't it be a lie, though?" she said. "I mean, even if I have a power like that, it can't just be a wand making people well? It sounds like... like magic."

"You're a nurse," he said. "Why do you think you chose that profession?"

She scoffed. "Oh, come on. Lots of people—" She stopped short, remembering how drawn she had felt to the idea of helping; of healing. How exhausting it had been, and how exhilarating.

Alex was nodding. "You can heal people too. Maybe minds and souls will be more difficult, but if you harness that power..."

"How?" she cried and made a helpless gesture. "Is it in books?"

"It must be. Yes, in some. But not instructions, I don't think."

"Then how would I even go about learning that? If that's what I can do?"

"I supposed that's the first step. Seeing if you are unique in that way. Doing some exercises to see whether you can heal, even without touching. That will help you start to find out."

"So what kind of exercises are we talking about?"

"Meditation. Kind of." He formed a pained, apologetic expression. "I learned this stuff as a kid, with my parents. That's what they did. They developed people's gifts. They taught us the exercises. Many top psychics went through there."

"I know they had a school, but it's closed now, right?"

"Yes. They passed away in an accident when we were still kids, so we let it go. My sisters and I still live there—it's been the family home for generations—but we don't teach."

"Why not?" she asked eagerly. "So many people must be like me, not knowing what they are and what to do."

"Yes, true. Of course. But though we know how to teach it, we just—it's hard—"

Sarah nodded. "But Alex, don't you see? You could help so many people. And wouldn't you find some meaning in this work?" She hesitated before she added, "Sometimes, when we suffer, if we give of ourselves, we can heal."

"Spoken like the door of light," he said with a sad laugh.

His sadness touched her. She felt the deep pain surrounding him. Maybe they could help each other.

"Won't you teach me?" she asked.

He frowned and looked out the window while slightly shaking his head. "It's not something you can learn in a day. It would take a lot of time. Maybe weeks. Or longer."

Sarah's job as a nurse popped into her mind, but she pushed the thought aside. She *did* have a special gift, and it had to do with healing—even her equally gifted grandmother had pointed that out on occasion. But there were other things to consider:

Finn, Emmie and the desire to help them—and the desire to help herself. To become herself. She had been in their shadow, with Emmie always so brave and determined, and Finn so brilliant and tortured. And now she knew she had something special, and had known since Whisper House. Whether or not it was this power Alex described, she needed to master it.

"I'll find the time," she said. "You had a school, right? You must have rooms there."

"Yes." Alex met her gaze.

"I can pay you."

Alex shook his head and threw up his hands, as if saying that was not needed. He had money, by the sound of it, and it was obvious that his family had been rich for a long time, and maybe his parents had never even charged their students.

"It's a calling, then," she said. "Isn't it? It's somehow what you would have done, had your parents lived?"

Drawing in a big breath, Alex let it out slowly, a frown pushing hard against his brow. "If you are... that—what I said—then you shouldn't let it go to waste. I think it's one in a generation, if that. And the thing is, once it starts happening, it just keeps appearing."

She nodded. "It shouldn't go uncontrolled. But are you saying that it can do harm?"

"I guess anything can." He nodded toward the water on the table. "Drink too much of that and you'll die."

A sense of responsibility, of destiny, hung over Sarah now. Maybe she was being silly; maybe it wasn't all that. But, somehow, she knew it was calling her.

"My sisters..." he said. "They live there; they're not very... social."

"That's all right," she said, half wanting to ask more and half knowing she needed to keep convincing him.

"They would never hurt anyone," he added quickly. "And we do have Wi-Fi and perfect phone reception." He thought a little more and added, "No TV, though."

She laughed. "Haven't watched it in ages."

"I can't guarantee that you *are* the door of light," he said, lowering his voice. "I can train you, whatever skills you have."

"And that's enough."

"All right," he said, and nodded once, as if further convincing himself. He looked up and smiled. "Will you bring your friends?"

"No."

He seemed startled.

"No," she repeated firmly. "This time I'll go alone."

❧ 6 ❧

A rriving at her home an hour later, Sarah sat on her bed with mixed feelings. She had loved her job, but this had the potential to multiply that by infinity.

She called her mom, who answered on the first ring. After the usual updates on her life, she broke into the real reason for her call. "Mom, I'm taking a trip."

"What? Alone?"

"Yes."

"What about Finn? And Emmie?"

"This one's for me. I just need time to myself for a while. It's just to St. Augustine, Florida. A friend of mine has a house there."

"That's a lot of cabin fever, Sarah," her mother joked. "Mexico and that house in the woods and now Florida?" But then her Mom's tone turned more serious. "What about your job?"

"I'm quitting."

There was silence on the line. She could feel her mother's anxiety even through the phone. "What about your health insurance and paying expenses?"

"It's just for a little while. I've got some money saved away and life is more than just nursing. I'll be all right."

After a moment, her mother sighed. "I guess I knew something like this was coming. You're just like your grandma. She went through moments like this too, taking off to *grow*, as she put it. I guess your grandmother would say that it's destiny."

"Yes," Sarah said. "That's just it. Destiny."

"I know you have to go. So much like her. But you need to make sure you have your benefits covered or leave some door open at work..."

"I will," Sarah said, knowing she might never return to nursing. She would develop this power and be even more of an asset to what she and Emmie had decided to do with their lives. They would work together, and somehow they would get by. That's what they had to do.

"Make sure to stay in touch or I'll worry." Her mother's voice wavered as if on the verge of tears. She was so full of worry already, but bravely accepting it.

"I will."

She ended the call, a heavy burden seemingly lifted from her shoulders with her mother's reluctant blessing. Next, she texted Emmie, relaying the same information she had given her mother about quitting her job and going to find herself.

Emmie texted back immediately: *I guess everyone's gotten that itch. Go and be free! Lots to share with you about Dr. Albright's death, but I'll save the details for a call later.*

Sarah: *Do you need my help?*

Emmie: *Jason and I are on it, and it might turn out that there's nothing we can do to help solve it anyway. Where are you going exactly?*

Sarah: *St. Augustine, Florida, this time. I can't afford fancy resorts like Finn. I'll be staying with a friend. Don't worry, I'll be fine! Really just need to recharge.*

Emmie: *Hugs.*

Sarah: *I've also been looking into telepathy as a way to communicate, and astral projections and all that.*

Emmie: *?????*

Sarah: *LOL. It's a whole thing. There's so much more to this whole psychic thing than we know, even with all the books. Or maybe it's in all the books.*

Emmie: *Well, yeah. Be careful where you tread. Death everywhere. We know that.*

Sarah: *Know it.*

Emmie: *You won't train without me, right?*

Sarah: *No! Just thinking.*

Emmie: *OK. Don't astral-visit me, please. Just text or call.*

Sarah: *LOL. I won't try. Might get lost.*

7

Emmie and Jason arrived at Dr. Albright's condo building by late afternoon, and Jason parked on the street just outside the entrance. A few scattered pedestrians walked around them beneath the shadows of the live oaks and palm trees that lined the street as they stared toward the property.

"It feels strange," Emmie said.

Jason looked at her. "You feel something already?"

"Not on a psychic level. Just a hunch."

Trees and shrubs partially shrouded the building. A row of barred windows along the bottom floor of the two-story construction was visible from where they had parked, and for some strange reason she expected to see Dr. Albright peering out from one of them.

"You're nervous," Jason said, touching her hand.

She squeezed his fingers. "It doesn't seem real, somehow, that he's gone and we're here at his home. I wasn't exactly pleasant when I ended my training with him, and now we're about to meet again under the worst of circumstances."

"I won't deny that it's disturbing. Are you having second thoughts?"

She shook her head. "No. I need to go in there." She exaggerated a wide grin.

He touched her cheek. "Yeah, you just keep doing that. That pretty smile of yours."

For the first time since she'd heard of Dr. Albright's death, she let out a little laugh within the thrill of his touch, but quickly tensed again as they stepped out of the car.

It only took a few minutes for them to walk around a tall brick wall that lined the edge of the property as they made their way toward the entrance. Jason stayed close to her, holding her hand and squeezing it gently as if to soothe her.

"They might not let us in." She looked at him. "Any ideas on how to get in there?"

"I'll just ask."

Despite Jason's confidence, a sense of unease persisted in her chest on a deeper level, like the impending dread she'd felt in her bedroom as a child knowing the Hanging Girl would make an appearance. Somehow, it had nothing to do with Dr. Albright at all. His death had unnerved her, but something wasn't right on a grander scale.

They followed the cement path up to the entrance and Jason pressed a lighted button on an intercom box near the door marked 'Building Manager.'

A minute later, a man's impatient voice answered, "Yes."

"Hi," Jason said. "We were students of Dr. Albert Albright. After what happened, we'd like to leave a flower in his place to honor him. Would you please let us in so we can grieve?"

There was a pause. "I'm sorry. The police ordered me not to let anyone in there. My condolences."

"That makes sense," Jason continued. "Can we leave it outside his door?"

"I can only allow tenants into the building at this time. The police gave me strict orders."

"I understand, but we've come a long way. My friend is particularly heartbroken. Would you mind delivering it to the doctor's door for her? You could do it yourself, just place it outside the door. It would mean a lot to her, considering this unthinkable tragedy."

Another pause. The man's voice came back a bit softened. "I suppose I could do that. Just a minute."

Emmie threw Jason a side-eyed glance. "I don't have a flower."

"Doesn't matter. Don't worry."

A short time later, a large balding man came to the door with a curious expression. He studied Jason, then Emmie, looking at her up and down. "Where's the flower?"

Jason leaned forward and stared at him through the glass. "I've got a better idea. You should let us in so we can look around for a while."

The man's reaction was at once subtle and quick. His face began brightening with a wide smile and wide eyes as he nodded. "That's a wonderful idea." He opened the door wide without giving Emmie a second glance.

As they stepped through the door, Emmie met his gaze and whispered, "What just happened?"

He looked a little guilty but shrugged. "I told you not to worry."

They followed the manager down a well-lit hallway to apartment 112. Before they arrived, a faint toxic smell filled the air. Not enough to sicken her, but enough to make her cringe.

It'll only get worse inside.

Someone had taped an official police notice to the door stating that entrance to the condo was not allowed and was subject to police arrest. The manager dismissed it with a wave of his hand. "It's all right if you look around for a while." He unlocked the door and ushered them inside.

"Thank you," Jason said, staring at the manager again. "That's very kind of you. You should leave us alone now for as long as we want. Just warn us if someone is coming. And you shouldn't tell the police or anyone that you ever saw us. In fact, you should forget you ever saw us."

The manager nodded several times. "Oh, absolutely. I'll leave you alone. Take your time!"

"Thank you," Jason repeated.

The manager shut the door behind himself as he left, and Emmie waited until his footsteps echoed down the hallway before saying anything.

"Did you do what I think you just did?" she asked.

"What do you *think* I just did?" His grin faded quickly as he rubbed his forehead.

"You pulled an old trick out of your hat? I thought you didn't do that stuff anymore."

Jason winced and stared at the floor. "I don't like to—definitely not—but... under the circumstances."

She stepped toward him. "Does it hurt?"

"A little, but as long as I don't use it often... I can manage."

"What happens when you use it too often?"

"Nothing good." He glanced toward the living room. "We should hurry."

She turned and faced the living room, and immediately spotted the recliner the news report had described as the place where they'd found Dr. Albright's body, or what was left of it.

Thousands of books filled the ceiling-high shelves around her. To say the old man had amassed a library was an understatement. It wasn't just a bookcase here or there; the doctor had transformed every inch of his home into a giant study with several small "stations" walled up with books around a small patch of space on every available surface. Bookcases were stacked atop other bookcases, with some of them angling forward as if they would crash down at any moment. Even the dining room table had been turned into a makeshift desk littered with stuffed folders, scattered papers and open books, leaving only a small space for sifting through them.

One large rolltop desk sat in the corner, almost buried

beneath more clutter. Each compartment was full of documents, letters and rolled up magazines.

Dr. Albright had been something of a hoarder, she supposed. A hoarder of knowledge, worse than Betty. Thank God Finn wasn't here, or he would have tried to put books in a suitcase to take them away...

As she stepped toward the doctor's recliner, a solemn feeling swept through her. Dr. Albright had *died* there. But she pushed aside her regret at the way he had met his death and focused on the task at hand. Just as she'd read earlier, there was no sign of extensive fire damage except for some light burn marks in the recliner and along the table beside it. Scattered ashes lightly dusted the floor, but that horrible, toxic smell... It overwhelmed her now—almost making her choke—as she glanced around the room. Something was definitely not right. Something was missing.

"He's not here," Emmie said.

Jason straightened and stepped toward her. "You don't see Dr. Albright?"

"No. But I do know he died here. I can feel that he did."

"But isn't that how things work? The spirits tend to remain where they died, right?"

Emmie nodded, then closed her eyes and focused. She *did* sense Dr. Albright's spirit had been there and was still somehow connected to that place, yet it was clear that he was gone. She opened her eyes again and looked at Jason. "I don't see him anywhere. But I *should* see him so easily, especially after all that happened."

"Where do you think he is?"

She tried to articulate her thoughts. "He's here... and not here. Maybe he went to another location, or someone took him?"

"Is that possible?" Jason examined a pile of books on a shelf across the room.

"I suppose it is, although I wouldn't say it's normal and I

don't know how that might happen. Spirits do roam sometimes, I guess, if someone leads them away."

He turned back toward her. "Well, you're the expert with the Third Eye, so whatever you say, I believe you."

Emmie partially closed her eyes to try again, straining to detect any spirits within the building or nearby as she made her way around the condo in a semi-meditative state. Ashes still remained scattered around the base of the chair and along the seat, but any remnants of Dr. Albright's body were gone, if any part of him had remained intact.

"If whatever or whoever burned him meant to destroy evidence, they couldn't have done a better job," Jason said. "I was told his computer is gone too. Burned, though the police have it."

Emmie stared at the blackened seat where Dr. Albright had sat for the last time. The outline of his body was there, like the ghostly remnants of a person vaporized in a nuclear blast, and near the center lay a darker circular shape almost hidden within the shadowy form. It wasn't immediately visible until she stopped trying to see it, like an optical illusion that forces you to change your focus to spot a hidden image within another one. "What's that?"

Jason stepped over and followed her gaze. "What's what?"

"On the chair. Do you see it?"

He was silent for a moment, tilting his head to one side. "The ashes?"

"Within the ashes. Some sort of a shape."

"Like what?"

"I don't know, like a... cinnamon roll."

Jason laughed briefly. "We'll stop at the coffee shop on the way out."

She rolled her eyes. "I'm serious. It's there."

He leaned in closer, then stepped back. "I do see it. I wonder if anyone else did."

Emmie grabbed her phone and took a photo of it, then

walked around and took several more photos of her surroundings. "Maybe I'll see something in them later. Sometimes a spirit doesn't appear right away. Where's Finn when you need him?"

Grabbing the phone, Jason zoomed into the photos she'd just taken, focusing on the darkened shape on the recliner. "Something is there, all right. I don't think this is just pareidolia either, where someone sees patterns in random shapes. I know someone who can help us track down what that means, if anything. A guy right here in New Orleans."

8

N ow Finn knew the truth. *His* truth.

No spirit had possessed him at Whisper House. Just pure, completely uninhibited Finn Adams.

Hold up a mirror, Finn. What do you see?

A killer.

But I didn't kill anyone.

He walked to Natalia's house for the second time. What could she *really* do for him? The doubt in his mind had only hardened into some horrible certainty that he was a monster, and he didn't know what a New Age-slash-Santería "good" witch could do about it.

The point was: He had threatened the lives of his friends at Whisper House, and how could he ever work with them again, be near them, risk a new appearance of the monster that lurked in him?

How could he face Sarah again? Sarah, who had shined so brightly that even *he* had felt her warm glow in that moment as the spirits passed through her. Emmie had called her the most beautiful thing she'd seen. So true.

The thought chilled him as he nodded at people walking his way, laughing, saying, *"Buenos días."* The woman of the fruit stand was there, under her umbrella. He moved left across the beach after removing his shoes. Today he'd been wiser and worn slip-on canvas shoes, breezy white trousers and a sandy-brown linen shirt. *Bet I still look like a damn gringo.* He towered over the Cubans and his face was a bit too red, but at least he wasn't dripping in sweat.

"Finn!" Natalia cried from her veranda as he approached.

Not too long ago, he would have thought she looked pretty good in a sundress buttoned in front, bare feet, soft black curls blowing all over the place. But what he felt today was more like: What the hell am I still doing here, *bruja?*

Still, her joy was contagious, and he returned her white smile as he approached. And then she whipped out a man's bathing suit from behind her back.

"You put this on and go swim."

He looked at the sea and then back at her. "What?"

"Go!"

"Is this some kind of spiritual bath? For purity or something?"

"No, Finn," she said, taking a step closer. "It's that I want to see your body."

He rolled his eyes. "Actually, I don't want to put on something that another wayward soul has been wearing."

"*Tonto,*" she said. "It is for purity. I mean, more like purification." She turned and moved toward the front door, adding, "Your aura is horrible. Like dark green and rotten. You need to go in salt water. Besides, I'm cooking."

Finn stood there and considered sending Jason a message loaded with expletives. Was this some sort of an elaborate joke? Had he wanted Finn out of the way, or was there anything at all to the Circe of Cuba?

But he ended up obeying her, after being assured by shouts from the kitchen that the bathing suit was cleaner than his conscience. As he ran into the sea, swam and then floated, he hoped he wouldn't get a lot of teasing and puns for nothing.

When he got back to the veranda, the damn woman had taken his clothes and not left a towel, so he had no choice but to walk to the kitchen all wet. The smell of fish and spices filled the air.

Natalia stirred a dish of vegetables that sizzled and crackled as steam billowed to the ceiling and dissipated like a puff of smoke. She turned to look at him as he stood dripping.

And actually did look him up and down.

"My clothes?" Finn sighed.

"Wow," she said, hand on one hip. "Your girlfriend must be missing you."

"She's not my girlfriend," he said repressively.

Natalia made a gesture over him. "She must be missing all this."

"Where are my clothes, Natalia?" he said, feigning patience.

She nodded toward the next room. "Go cover yourself, player."

He went to the room and saw a towel laid out for him, and his clothes. After drying and dressing, he took out his phone and looked at his messages. Nothing from Sarah. A flash of pain swept through his heart. She also had gone somewhere to find herself, Emmie had told him.

As far from me as possible, probably.

His finger hovered over the keypad as he considered writing a message to her, but instead he left her profile and went to Emmie's. She had been silent too, and now Finn typed: *I'm in Cuba while some New Age crystal-and-cymbals woman is cooking me lunch. I have a lot to say to your boyfriend, by the way. But I guess I'll wait to scream it in person.*

He was going to put the phone away in his pocket when it buzzed. A message from Emmie. Hell, she typed fast.

Emmie: *You won't believe this, but we are in the middle of another murder.*

Finn: *What?????*

Emmie: *You know Dr. Albright? I talked about him. Mean old guy who used to train me and Jason? Was found burnt to death here in New Orleans. At his home. Weird stuff.*

Finn: *Our kind of weird stuff?*

Emmie: *Yes. Sort of. Not normal fire. Burned some stuff and not the rest, and he was big in the psychic community. Like an association. Carey Kali, it's called.*

Finn: *Death seems to follow you...*

Emmie: *Funny. How do you know it doesn't follow you too?*

Finn: *What are you going to do?*

Emmie: *We're trying to find out more.*

Finn felt the rush of adrenaline. The excitement of a new case, the impulse to do what he loved and the knowing that he needed to be there. He glanced back toward the door. What *was* he doing there? He had to leave. Somehow. No time for swimming or eating cilantro. But then again, he shouldn't be around Emmie, much as she had forgiven him for trying to kill her...

He typed: *Keep me informed. Seriously, this doesn't sound like your typical arsonist. Be careful. Don't burn.*

Emmie: *I won't. And you watch out for... crystals... and cymbals... Very dangerous.*

Finn: *Har-Har.*

When he entered the kitchen again, smoothing his wet and salty hair, Natalia said, "Your friends are quite busy in New Orleans."

It seemed she was now making mojitos.

"Where did you hear that?" he asked.

"Jason sent a message. Dr. Albright's death was unexpected."

"Do all of you psychics have a Gossip Group Chatroom or what?"

She played along. "Something like that."

Finn scoffed. "Of course."

Natalia handed a glass to him and clinked hers against it.

"Thought this was for your orishas," he said. He looked in the glass. "Any purity in here?"

"Stuff that gets rid of purity faster than anything," she teased.

At his face, she snapped her tongue. "Ay, Finn, don't be boring. Go sit down."

She had set the table her way. Dishes and cutlery thrown around over a colorful tablecloth. As he sat, she carried over the food to the heavy wooden table and made herself comfortable beside him.

"Did you know him?" he asked as she put food on his dish without asking how much he wanted.

"The doctor? No, I never met him. I managed to elude training from their organization, Carey Kali, unlike Jason."

Finn shook his head and laughed. "That name... Makes their group sound like a sorority based on an Indian goddess."

"You're not so far off."

He began to eat as she talked. The food was delicious, but he often paused to take in what she was saying.

"Carey Kali are the rationalists of the psychic world, you could say. Basically, they have thought for over a hundred and fifty years that all the power shouldn't be out there willy-nilly and started trying to lay down the law." She grimaced and sipped her mojito. "They wanted everyone to be secret about it, like some mafia thing, and go to meetings where they'd tell others what they could and couldn't do. They were like corporate meetings, though, as opposed to backroom type of thing, with nametags and coffee in paper cups. That kind of nonsense. Or so I've been told; I never went."

"And what *could* people do or not do according to them?"

She laughed, then made a harsh face. "Nothing! You will do nothing!"

Finn threw her a wry look. "And you didn't like that. Because you're a free spirit."

She narrowed her eyes and leaned away from him, her skirt rising to show more of her legs than Finn cared to see. "Nobody can tell me what to do. What's the point of getting a gift from the gods and not using it?" She sat upright again and tapped her chest dramatically. "I had a gift, and I was damn well going to find out all I could about it and develop it. I knew what I could do, heal people, and I knew I could do it very well."

"So that's what you can do..."

"You want a resume or what?"

"Are you saying nobody trained you?"

"That's the thing. I did spend some time at one of the smaller places to develop my skills, in a way I could shine..." She stared off, as if remembering.

"How did that go?" Finn asked.

"Let's just say..." She seemed to be trying to find the right words before speaking, which was unlike what he had seen of her so far. "Let's just say I saw the point of some control. A give-and-take sort of thing. I was a teen at the time, training in this place with a bunch of others, and it got weird. If Carey Kali was too conservative, this place was way too ambitious and... wild."

He tried not to choke on his mojito. "Too wild for *you*?"

"I know it's hard to believe." She raised her arms and waved her hands, her bracelets jangling. "Wrong kind of wild, *guapo*. I learned a lot of things, then adapted them to me. That's the most important thing, you see, being oneself." Apparently unable to stay still, she now leaned forward and put a hand under the table. "Like you should be yourself."

She touched his knee and he recoiled.

"Listen, Natalia," he said, "I don't know how much of what you say is kidding, but it's better if I just state that I'm going to keep my rotten, frustrated aura for a while."

A slow smile crept over her face. "Loyal to your girlfriend. I like that."

"She's not—" He put down his fork, picked up his glass and, leaning back, he took a big gulp from it. "What is it that you can do for me? Why don't you just tell me?"

"I needed to see you for a bit in order to know."

"Like to see me in a bathing suit?"

Her laugh was a giggle now, and it ended up making him giggle too.

"Have you thought, at any time, that you wanted to strangle me?" She got up and went behind the kitchen counter, where she began to mix more mojitos.

"Are you serious?"

"Yes! Have you thought, 'What a pain this woman. I want to shake or strangle her.'"

He shrugged. "Maybe." Where was this going?

She cut a lemon as she kept on speaking. "Imagine that thought gets stopped in the flux of things. Instead of slipping away, like air, it stays there. Crystalizes. Gets encrusted in your brain."

Turning serious, Finn listened to her. "Go on."

"We have thoughts like that. Hundreds of thousands or more thoughts a day. Some micro ones, you don't even know they went through your brain. Then an entity, more powerful than you, takes over. Maybe it's in your head a while, finding those thoughts, making them bigger, pounding on them. Drawing them out." She turned the wooden pestle, crushing the lemon one way and then the other, as if those were the thoughts she was talking about. "They might have been so unimportant you didn't even register them. A flash of irritation at just about anything which gets pulled, manipulated, blown up. It's like your brain becomes a furnace, except someone else is making metal in there. Iron and steel."

She walked over with the pitcher and refreshed their drinks, sitting down again. Finn had been incapable of saying a word, just taking in what she was saying, remembering his red-hot thoughts at Whisper House. Being blown up and twisted by a little boy who also knew anger.

"You're condemning yourself without a proper trial, and that's just as wrong as pretending you're a saint," she said. "You were a victim of a stronger force, something that preyed on you. The thoughts were you, yes. And they are in me, and in anyone you can think of." She stared at him for a second and then added, "You love your friend, Finn. You love a woman too. Very much, or you wouldn't be here, and you wouldn't be suffering."

Setting down her glass, she continued.

"Even I could take that guilt, that suffering, and torture you with it. Make it stay in your mind, and grow and grow, and take over like a fungus. But you are so good at doing it yourself."

"All right," he said after a moment. "I get the... concept. But what am I doing here now? What can I do about it?"

"You want to be with your friends and still work with them. I saw how excited you got about the old man dying. See? You could dwell on that thought. *I'm so happy an old man was burned to death.* But that's not what it is. You just love being a team with your friends, but you are scared of yourself and of the psychic world. And I'm here to show you there are ways to engage in the psychic world, ways to face it, even *embrace* it, without worrying about losing control of yourself."

"I can't hurt my friends," he told her.

"Oh, don't be so self-obsessed. The psychic world is all around us all the time. Some in it already know you, probably. Some will get to you through memories or feelings in your friends. So there is no running from it, but you can learn to know your enemy, Finn, which is everywhere. You can learn to protect yourself."

Only weeks before, he would have jumped at the chance. Now... "I don't know that I can play in that league."

"You think you're the only one who has ever had a problem like this?"

He took another sip of his drink and stared out the window at the placid blue sky. "I didn't think there was such a horrible side to myself. I always thought I was just a run-of-the-mill psycho at times, not a murderer."

"You're traumatized and still exaggerating. There's plenty we can do. You just need some training to empower yourself and see that you cannot only protect your friends but actively do some good in their lives. Don't you think they miss you too?" She ran her eyes over his body again. "That girl of yours?"

"Is it magic?" he countered quickly. "What you do?"

She snorted. "Magic?"

"I know it exists. Dark magic too. Bring me my loved one and all this shit."

"No, Finn. It's not like that."

"The herb stuff and—"

"I'm a healer. That's what I do. And there are different ways to heal. There are different ways to understand psychic phenomena. I've been talking to you and watching you and seeing your aura—which isn't rotten, by the way. It's tortured. There's also a lot of light in it, but it's churning in there and being held back. And my conclusion is you need to protect yourself. Even from yourself. You need to know how."

Sarah came to his mind, laughing inside the sea, beautiful, trusting, and happy. He longed to see her like that again, but he would need to make sure no feelings of his—that anger, always there—might be manipulated by any psychic phenomena.

Natalia stretched her hand over the table. "Take my help."

"If I do, I need you to promise me something," Finn said, placing the drink on the table.

"What's that?"

"Promise me that I will never be possessed like that again. Promise me—I'll never hurt them."

She took his hand. "I promise."

9

Sarah had read somewhere that St. Augustine was the oldest continuously inhabited city in America and judging by everything she saw as she drove through the small city, she had no doubt that it was true. The streets were lined with live oaks and historical mansions that must have stood for centuries judging by their dated structures. The narrow side streets and quaint residences still kept the same design aesthetics of a forgotten era of European occupation. Not a single modern house in sight.

She followed the directions of her phone's GPS to the far side of the city, coming around a line of trees and turned down a narrow paved road with signs posted on both sides stating that she was entering private property and there was no trespassing.

Sarah slowed the car when Temper House came into view at the end of the road. The house was set off behind several towering live oaks that stretched upwards and fanned out like an old man's bony fingers jutting toward the sky. A neck-high brick wall circled the property where the road ended, which was capped along the top with white masonry. A massive ornate iron gate blocked the road ahead and she stopped in front of it, pausing to scan the property.

Like the other houses in St. Augustine, this one was a historic mansion but didn't seem as old as the others. She had imagined that Temper House would resemble a grandiose mansion with Roman pillars accenting dramatic designs that would awe all visitors. But instead, the home more closely resembled an old college dormitory with a squarish main entrance centered between two wings that spread out on either side, dotted with evenly spaced windows staring back at her like watchful eyes.

They used to train psychics here, after all. Definitely not a tourist attraction.

A circular driveway wound around a marble water fountain in front of the entrance. The water wasn't flowing, but a bronze statue of a Hindu goddess stood in the center with several arms stretched out in all directions, her tranquil face staring forward as if meditating.

As Sarah slowed in front of the gate, she spotted a silver box and pulled up beside it, expecting that she would need to get buzzed in or call Alex to come out to get her. Instead, the gate clanked and creaked open. She drove onto the property as the gate snapped shut behind her.

Her phone rang at almost the same time. Alex's name popped up on the screen and she answered it while trying to navigate through the gate.

"Great to have you," he said. "Just come in and drive up to the door. Don't worry about where you park."

"Got it."

He hung up, and a moment later she spotted him standing at the entrance as he slipped the phone into his pocket. Alex was dressed in another suit, this time of navy-blue flannel, but he wore no tie today. She supposed it was his casual look—as casual as he would get. He didn't seem a vain man, but his golden locks and his suits and crisp shirts did give him a look of those old paintings she had seen more often since meeting Emmie and Finn. A man from another time; the tragic survivor from a few tragedies and the heir of a line that must have been distinguished in their world.

He waved as she followed the paved driveway around the water fountain and parked to the side near the grass.

She turned off the car and glanced out through the passenger side window, but he was already coming around to the driver's side.

"A home away from home," she said under her breath, echoing the way Alex had described it in a text earlier.

Before she could open the door, he opened it for her.

"Sarah," he said, "it's so wonderful that you're here."

She climbed out of the car. "Thank you."

They embraced for a moment before she stepped back and glanced toward the house. The details were hidden behind oak trees, but the overall Victorian style was clear, although it blended together with a heavy southern charm in a white and cream color scheme. It had been either a school or a hotel, without a doubt, and it branched off in both directions from a bold front entrance accented within an arched stone frame. White curtains covered every window and shallow porches shielded them on both levels, although they only extended over the front two windows on either side.

He gestured to the suitcase in the back seat of her car. "May I?"

Before she could answer, he'd opened the car door and lifted out the largest of the two suitcases she'd brought with her.

Sarah pulled out the other suitcase. "Have many psychics passed through here?"

"Not a huge number. But I think big in quality. My parents knew talent."

Her eyes widened as she looked around. "This is like a tropical paradise for someone from Minnesota in December. It was two degrees below zero when I left."

She glanced around the front yard. Live oak trees towered against the far corners of the property, with only thick swamps beyond that on both sides. No other cars in the driveway either.

"Are we the only ones here?" she asked.

He laughed. "No, thank goodness. I could never take care of all this myself. The groundskeeper stops by each day and my sisters hardly ever leave, so the cars are in the garage on the other side. And then there is the zoo."

"Oh yes! I read about the zoo."

Alex grinned as they walked side by side toward the entrance. "Out back. I'll give you a tour."

A light breeze passed over her face and she smelled the damp, swampy air. She spotted the source beyond the edge of the property. Thick grass and trees just after the fence. Something moved in the grass.

"Are there alligators around here?" she asked.

He laughed and tipped his head sideways. "Gators are everywhere in Florida, but we take great care, also to protect our animals. If you look at the fence all round our perimeter, it's built to be sturdy and not let them in. So there is nothing to worry about."

"But alligators are around."

"You'll forget your fears after a bit."

When they reached the entrance, Alex rushed ahead to open the door for her.

Yes, a gentleman... like Finn. A pang of emotional pain surged through her chest. She missed Finn intensely now, and meeting Alex's gaze, she saw he was aware of her conflict.

"You're already homesick," he said simply.

"I just haven't traveled alone much."

He led her into the house. "Then it's a bit of an adventure."

"Absolutely. And I did throw myself at you. I mean, at your house."

"Not in the least."

After stepping through the front door, she set down her suitcase and glanced around. She had arrived. No turning back, and whatever happened, whatever difficulties she faced from that point on, she would need to face them without her friends. Not that she needed anyone; she had power, and she knew it. And it would be an adventure, as Alex had said—no doubt about that.

The sound of chimes echoed from somewhere in the house, but rose and faded as she glanced around. The entryway opened to a larger hall full of antiques and paintings, but unlike Caine House, her surroundings were soothing. Vases brimming with roses sat in front of two windows as the sun streamed in, reflecting off the stained wood floors. The furniture and art were an eclectic mix of the traditional with a modern flair.

An assortment of weapons that appeared more ornamental than functional was displayed in glass cases along the wall: a dagger with a gold handle dotted with gems, and a matching sword against a red velvet background. They bore inscriptions and carved flowers and birds. A small metal antique cage, such as one might use to catch a small animal, sat perched on a marble pedestal in the corner, with the door open as if waiting to ensnare its prey.

"I believe my grandfather owned that," Alex said, seeing her study it. "During the height of our successes at Temper House, he used it to catch some of the smaller animals for snake food. He had a python at one time."

Sarah glanced at him nervously. "Not anymore, right?"

He smiled reassuredly. "Definitely not. I think we should go out back and take that tour of the zoo. If anything, it should ease your mind before you get settled into your room."

Alex took Sarah out to the back of the house, and she was astonished to encounter a sprawling yard full of statues and a lush garden. A winding stone path led out to what looked like small colorful palaces spread out among the trees and were in fact cages. None of the animals were visible from where she stood, but the noises they made drifted clearly to her: the gurgle and song of birds, the call of monkeys, and loud purring.

Alex walked her toward the painted domes atop large cages,

staying beside her every step of the way. "There's nothing to be afraid of. All of them are in the cages. They don't get visitors often anymore, so they will most likely be more afraid of you than you are of them."

The sun beamed across the green grass as they walked out through the garden and passed more statues that resembled gods and goddesses, some of them painted in colors and others made of marble and bronze.

Approaching the zoo compound, she saw a clear connection between the statues she had just passed and the structures housing the animals. They had built each cage like an Indian palace. "Your family followed the Eastern religions?"

"Not followed, as such, but my great-great-grandfather lived in India for a time and fell in love with its beauty and philosophy for life. He was Scottish but traveled a lot in the trade industry where he made his fortune, and he tried to bring some of that beauty with him when he started Temper House."

They arrived at the first animal. Parvati, as the nametag said, the orangutan. The creature's enclosure was a cylindrical, ornately painted structure like the others, with an ornamental roof. A wired fence enclosed it on all sides. The creature gave no reaction as Sarah approached, watching her carefully as it sat against a stripped tree stump.

"She's not too keen on visitors, I'm afraid. She's been sad since her mate died a while ago."

Sarah read the plaque next to Parvati's, which someone had partially crossed out. "Shiva."

Sarah met Parvati's gaze and sensed its curiosity at her presence but also the orangutan's sorrow.

"Oh. Poor darling. Shouldn't she be in a bigger enclosure?"

"You don't need to feel sorry. They're born in captivity, and if we had just let them loose, they wouldn't have survived. As their numbers dwindle, we will eventually close all this down, but until then, it's our duty to care for them."

Sarah glanced around at some of the other cages. Many of them were empty. "So all of these were full at one time?"

"It was quite popular a hundred years ago after my family constructed it, but back then and even after, people weren't so... finicky. Not about animals anyway. Certainly not even about people." He gave her a bright smile. "But it's different now, of course, and we treat them well, as you can see. They've inherited the family fortune as much as we did."

Alex led her out past a few more cages, passed a tiger and later on a pair of giraffes standing beside a small pond where a group of flamingos huddled while watching them. Beyond that was a massive cage that Alex explained belonged to several species of birds: some parrots, an Eastern screech owl, two ostriches, a few macaws, a cockatiel, a rainbow lorikeet and peacocks. The plaques outside two other cages nearby revealed they held a puma and two black panthers sleeping atop a large stone outcropping surrounded by a grassy growth. Well-worn paths led down to a small cement channel of water running through the center of the cage. On the trees high above them, not enclosed in any cage, sat a hawk and a flock of smaller birds that chirped and shifted within the branches as they passed through.

The property sprawled farther than she had first thought. There was even a manmade brook running through it and extending as far as she could see. A couple of small bridges over it along the way featured statues standing guard on either side. More Hindu gods that Sarah didn't recognize. Finn would have known their names.

"My great-great-grandfather, Lennox Temper, built everything, bringing in species from all over the world, including some local ones. I was told it was a magnificent place to visit in its heyday."

Sarah nodded, but it was making her sad to see so many captive animals, beautiful as the place might be. "It's... impressive."

"And a lot of work." Alex gestured back to the house. "I think now you've seen some of this, you're ready to settle into your room and get a little rest before supper. I just wanted to give you a glimpse of Temper House history."

Sarah nodded politely. "Thank you."

Despite the animals, the smell was not too bad, most likely due to the abundant flowers that grew beside each enclosure. Many roses of different colors. If the purpose of the zoo had been to bring a sense of wonder and peace to visitors, then it had succeeded. Sarah closed her eyes for a moment and took in all the small sounds around her. The rustling of the leaves overhead, the cracking branches from a tree nearby, and the little animal noises that filled the air. The place was alive in every sense of the word.

"Can you feel it?" Alex asked. "The life in this space."

"I can."

"It was always meant to represent the cycle of life, death and rebirth. Like the Indian gods too." Alex touched her arm. "Let's get you to your room."

He led Sarah back into the house, grabbing both suitcases near the door where they'd left them earlier, then led her up the staircase toward the right wing of the building. At the top of the stairs, she glanced over to her left. Most of the lights were off.

"Are there rooms on both sides?" she asked.

Alex stopped and followed her gaze. "There are. My sister mostly takes care of that side, and she likes to keep it the way things used to be. It's where the school was."

Sarah nodded and followed Alex to the right down a short hallway, arriving at a room that looked over the garden where they had just walked. The room was clean and well-lit, with modern furniture, a laptop, plenty of books, and even more roses. He had prepared for her arrival with care, and she was grateful.

"After you get unpacked, come down. I'll be cooking the meal tonight, but Lorelei is a bit of a stickler on keeping to a schedule. Six p.m., exactly. That's when you can meet my sisters."

"Great."

Alex glanced around the room. "Nobody will enter here without your permission, and whenever you need it cleaned, the groundskeeper's wife will take care of it."

"Thank you."

"I think you'll find the accommodations more comfortable than any hotel in the area."

Alex left the room, leaving Sarah to unpack. She went through a few things, moving them into two of the empty dresser drawers, but stopped when someone's voice caught her ear. It was coming from one of the rooms nearby. A woman's voice. A singsong flow of words that she couldn't quite make out, like a child's playful rhyme.

One of Alex's sisters?

She walked over to the door and pressed her ear against it. The voice was louder, and she could make out the words now.

Love is patient. Love is kind.

10

Sarah opened her bedroom door and peeked her head out into the hallway, cautiously at first, as if she were doing something forbidden. The woman's soft voice was lovely, almost childlike. It was coming from a room not too far away and the door was wide open.

She moved forward slowly, each step creaking against the old wooden floorboards even as the red carpeting that covered most of the walkway failed to dampen the noise. Alex *had* told her that she could go anywhere, so she really didn't need to creep around.

Straightening her posture, she stepped toward the melodic voice.

"Love is patient. Love is kind. Love is patient. Love is kind."

She could feel the woman's emotions behind the words. A prayer? Someone missing a loved one... like me?

She stopped at the open doorway. A section of the wall blocked her from seeing the source of the words coming from around a corner just inside the door. The room was pristine and girlish, and a soapy smell filled the air, as if someone had just taken a shower. Even as Sarah stood in the doorway, leaning forward to find the source of the singing, the woman continued repeating the same phrase.

"Hello?" Sarah asked softly. "I don't mean to interrupt..."

The voice stopped suddenly. Something metallic knocked against wood as if the person had dropped an object, and after some rustling and a few grunts, a woman's face appeared ahead, peering around the corner. Her blond wet hair hung in straight clumps and her eyes were wide as she silently met Sarah's gaze.

"I just heard your song and I wanted to say hi. My name is Sarah. You must be one of Alex's sisters?"

The woman stared blankly from the door of her ensuite bathroom. The resemblance to Alex was clear: she had the same jawline and sweet, thoughtful gray eyes.

Sarah heard nothing, but she felt a sudden presence behind her. She looked over her shoulder and another woman stood leaning against the door. Her hair fell to her shoulders in a blunt cut, and she wore a fringe almost to her eyes. Gray eyes, but her hair was black as midnight. Alex and the singing woman had soft, pink lips, but this woman had a wide mouth, currently curved on only one side in a smile that wasn't very welcoming. But she was a striking figure with a healthy body, curvy and slim at the same time, which was accented by tight jeans and a clinging sweater. Her feet were bare, her nails painted dark red.

The woman spoke in a hoarse, deep voice, "You must be Sarah. The only person we're expecting this year."

Sarah gave an uncertain smile. "Yes. And you're Alex's other sister? You all have the same eyes."

"Not the same..." the woman said, ungluing herself from the doorframe and walking into the room. She offered her hand to her sister, who took it and seemed to slide and thump forward.

Sarah's gaze jumped to the photo on the wall: the three siblings, with the blonde woman standing straight and laughing into the camera. In the photo, she looked so happy and healthy. Yet Sarah could recognize the victim of a stroke in the awkward gait and the curled hand, with one leg twisted at an odd angle.

"There, Cecilia," the sister said, more kindly than she had

said anything until now. Her sharp features had softened too. "This isn't really an intruder. She wanted to meet you."

Sarah's face warmed. "I heard the singing and thought I'd introduce myself. Her voice sounded so... beautiful."

"She sings quite a bit." The woman gave a wry smile. "Better get used to it. I'm Lorelei, by the way."

"You're the... older sister?"

"Oldest of the bunch."

Sarah did a quick calculation in her mind. If Lorelei was the oldest, then she must be in her mid-thirties, with Alex maybe a year or two younger. That put Cecilia in her late twenties. A flash of sympathy swept through her. So young for a stroke victim.

Cecilia spoke softly, almost as a whisper, "Love is patient..."

"That's in the Bible... I think," Sarah said. She remembered some of it: *Love is patient, love is kind. It does not envy, it does not boast, it is not proud... It always protects, always trusts, always hopes...*

Lorelei grinned. "She's not a religious nut or anything. It's the family motto. Love is patient." She stroked her sister's wet hair. "My sister went mad. Too much death."

Mad? Had the stroke incapacitated her mentally too?

Lorelei kissed Cecilia, walked past Sarah and stepped into the hallway. She gestured for Sarah to follow her.

They left Cecilia, who was now looking out the window, and walked down the hallway toward Sarah's room but kept going past it.

"You're a long way from home," Lorelei said.

"That's true. Minnesota."

Lorelei nodded. "Alex told me that he planned to train you."

"We'll try to see what I am."

"But you're an empath, though; correct?"

"Yes."

A wave of pain swept through Sarah's chest and head, and she curled forward. A million needles jabbed at her from all directions as if she had stuck her finger into an electrical outlet. It faded as quickly as it had arrived, but before it left her, she followed the source of her pain to the darkened area on the opposite wing. Within the shadows, a massive set of double doors sat at the end of the hallway.

Lorelei leaned forward and stared at her with what seemed like piercing curiosity. "You feel something?"

Sarah didn't answer, couldn't answer, as she struggled to regain her focus. She clenched her teeth for several seconds until the pain was gone. "I don't know what just happened."

Sarah stared at the double doors. Whatever had passed through her had come from behind those doors. "I'm just curious," Sarah said, "but what's in that room at the end of the hallway?"

"The old part. I know Alex told you that you're free to go anywhere in the house, but if you decide to explore that section, you go in there at your own peril. We didn't fix that part. Bad floors, bad ceilings, bad... everything."

Sarah glanced around at the modern light fixtures overhead, then down at the fresh carpeting and obvious renovations to the walls and ceiling. *Why would someone have such a lovely house and not fix half of it?*

She didn't ask.

11

For the first time, Natalia led Finn upstairs to a room devoid of all furniture. The room was dark, as black draperies covered the walls and windows. She switched off the single exposed light above them and lit several candles that were sitting along shelves in the corners of the room. A thick sandy area rug covered most of the floor, and she gestured for him to sit in the middle.

"Make yourself comfortable," she said.

He'd been there three times now, except this time she hadn't joked or made conversation. She had made her diagnosis, he supposed, and now they would begin what she called his training. He couldn't help feeling some anxiety at all the blackness; being buried alive had left him with more than a touch of claustrophobia, and the place was hot without a breeze. But he wiped his palms on his trousers and waited.

"Before we start"—Finn raised his hand—"we aren't going to conjure any spirits, are we? I haven't had a good track record with that."

Natalia scoffed. "Nothing like that. Take a moment to meditate, clearing your mind, and... relax."

He tensed at the way she said *relax.*

Watching him from the doorway for a moment, she smiled as if to assure him everything would be all right. "I'll get my things."

After she left, he sat on the rug as the scent of the candles filled the room with a sweet smell that did help to calm him a little. He took a deep breath of the quiet, still air and reminded himself that she was a professional at this, after all, and nothing *really* bad could happen.

Right?

Natalia returned a few minutes later carrying a hand-carved wooden tray loaded with items that resembled an odd tea set. She sat down facing him on the floor, the boards squeaking with their every movement, and carefully removed the items from the tray, laying them out between them in some sort of order that made no sense to him but seemed important to her. She filled the two black porcelain bowls with a thick black liquid that she poured from a silver teacup, then mixed in leaves that she crushed in another wooden bowl.

Smoke rose from the concoction, and she handed him one of the bowls. "Don't drink it; you need to breathe it all in."

The smell was bitter, but he did as he was told. Inhaling deeply over the smoke rising from the liquid, he cringed and then shuddered. Some of it spilled out over the edge of the cup and dripped onto the tray. "That's nasty."

"It's what you need."

Nausea spread through his chest. "We should've done this before I ate."

She seemed not to hear him, but instead gestured to his cup and stirred the bits of leaves. "Stare into the liquid. We're going to be reciting some phrases to practice connecting with someone on the outside, anyone at all, but whoever you decide, that's who you'll see within the blackness just as a psychic would see them. It doesn't mean you're psychic. It's all natural, a first step on this winding road. The knowledge itself that you'll witness isn't good or bad, it's just knowledge. How we choose to use it is up to us."

"Got it." Finn stared into the swirling black sludge and saw nothing.

"Whoever appears, don't let your mind wander into strong emotions, but try to look at them objectively watching them as a stranger would without attachment, if you can."

"All right. I understand."

She looked at him for a moment, then gazed into the bowl in her lap. "And don't worry about it if you don't see anything clearly the first time."

Finn did as she did. He swirled the black liquid counterclockwise, feeling a hint of hypnotic tranquility passing through him. Finally, she told him to stop. They recited the words she gave him several times in unison until she fell silent and he continued, waiting for the ripples in his liquid to settle. The glassy surface reflected the antique light fixture centered on the white ceiling above them.

He could only think of Sarah, and the emotions associated with her welled up inside him despite her insistence that he avoid it.

"Your breathing is shallow," she said. "You're too attached to your target. Take deep breaths and look objectively."

He did as she said and a minute later his mind was clearer.

"Do you see the person?" she asked.

He didn't, not at first, but the shapes and lines that he assumed were shadows and reflections in the liquid began to move in an unnatural way. The images coalesced and formed the vague semblance of Sarah's face and neck and hair. Her smile widened then faded as a line of black liquid moved down and crossed her neck like an arm preparing to pull her in.

Finn's heart beat faster. He strained to see her with more clarity as his hands trembled, obscuring the images with ripples that only made things worse. He tried to steady his hands, but her face stretched long as her eyes widened and her mouth opened in a silent scream. Was this just his imagination?

"Is this real?" His tense voice cracked. "What am I seeing here?"

"We can't be sure yet. It's most likely an impression of how your subject is in this moment."

"Someone's hurting her."

"Stay objective." Natalia looked down into his bowl. "It might appear that way."

He grumbled. "I don't like it."

"Don't take anything you see as literal. Many times you'll see disturbing images, but they are not revealing things exactly as they're happening, like I said. They're an impression of your target's reality. It takes some time to interpret them. That's why I recommend looking at them as you would look at a stranger."

"I... I can't do that." His hands were shaking more as the images of Sarah faded into nothingness within the black rippling liquid that now splashed against the sides of the bowl and dripped across his fingers and onto the rug beneath them. "What's happening to her?"

"It's okay." Natalia spoke in a soothing voice, reaching over and touching his hand.

He flinched when her fingers touched him and more liquid splashed over the side of the bowl, but another face appeared in the liquid, staring back at him—as clear as if he were staring into a mirror.

Neil.

His brother was just as Finn remembered him before the suicide, but there was someone standing over Neil, a dark entity that loomed behind him like a shadow ready to pounce. The tension spread through Finn's whole body, until the bowl slipped from his hands and cracked down against the tray, splashing the liquid across his legs and lap and her dress.

Natalia lurched back with a restrained cry. "*Santa María...*"

"You're just drugging me, aren't you?" Finn tried to shake off the images that still reverberated through his mind. "It's just a trick to mess with my mind."

"I didn't make you see anything," Natalia said. "You saw it alone. What did you see?"

"You're a phony, aren't you?" He tried to stand but lost his balance and dropped to the floor again. "What's in that shit? Mescaline? Magic mushrooms?"

She shook her head, making wide gestures that he should stay seated. "Other leaves."

He finally managed to stand by clutching one of the tapestries hanging from the wall to balance himself and made his way toward the door.

She reached toward him. "It's not safe for you to leave yet."

"It sure as hell isn't safe to stay."

"Take my hand."

As she tried to approach him, he pushed her away. "Don't touch me, you con artist. I knew you were a fraud as soon as I met you."

"Please stay calm."

"*Órale!*" He gestured her away.

Was the room spinning? He pulled at the buttons on his shirt in a panic. The heat was suffocating him. Natalia's words blurred together, and he clutched at anything in the darkness as his heart raced faster.

Later, he would not know how he got down the stairs, onto the street, and much less to his hotel room. But that's where he woke—to find out a full day had passed in a dark and dreamless sleep.

12

The smell of freshly cooked food filled the air as Sarah stepped down the stairs. She guessed it was Italian food judging by the scent of garlic and pasta and spices.

The dining room table came into view near the bottom of the stairs, just off to the left. The dining table was made of some high-quality wood like mahogany or cherry, with intricately carved details along the edges. There were six chairs upholstered in rich red velvet with button-tufted backs and decorative nail-head trim. A three-layer chandelier hung over the table and a large china cabinet sat against one wall. It was open, and some of the china pieces were missing. Sarah found them neatly placed at the table.

Alex was busy shuttling food and eating utensils back and forth from the kitchen. The steaming hot dishes and plates of desserts crowded the center of the table. She stopped at the bottom of the stairs and watched him.

He smiled at her. "Just a few more minutes."

"I can help."

He shook his head. "We've got everything taken care of." He paused and straightened as his expression turned somber. "Also, I just wanted you to know it's the fifteen-year anniversary of the death of my parents."

Sarah's eyes widened. "Oh, I'm sorry. I should have—"

Lorelei appeared carrying an armful of white roses, and she grinned at Sarah as she passed in front of her. "Brought flowers?"

Sarah didn't answer.

Lorelei continued across the room, carrying the roses toward the portrait of a middle-aged man and woman, then placed the vase in front of the portrait while touching the image and whispering something as if in prayer. She pushed her eyes closed for several seconds, then opened them suddenly and turned.

The resemblance between her and her father was striking. He was a tall, sharp-featured man, serious and imposing. Her siblings had taken after the mother, a blonde woman with a clear gaze and a kind smile.

All three of them had inherited their father's eyes. In Lorelei, however, the gray seemed like a wintry sky.

"You're staring," Lorelei said, amused.

"I'm sorry."

"Do you say that a lot?" Lorelei walked past her, not looking at Sarah. "Bet you do."

I'm not sorry, then.

Alex *had* given her fair warning that the sisters were not easy. One was a recluse who worshipped her dead parents, apparently, and the other was ruined in her youth by a cruel, silent medical condition.

Alex had joined her by the portrait. "They died not long after this was commissioned. The accident came as a shock, I guess, as all accidents do. They were the driving force in attracting undeveloped psychics here and training them, and we were too young to do the same."

The portraits around the area caught Sarah's gaze again, and together they followed the lineage from Alex's parents backwards. Something was missing.

Alex's dead wife and child. No sign of them anywhere. Her heart ached for him. He *had* seen a lot of tragedy.

When she met Alex's gaze, he gave no indication of knowing what she was thinking and gestured toward a hallway. "We'll take the long way back to the dining room."

He led her down the long, spacious, well-lit hallway with a row of three doors on the left side—and between doors hung deliberately arranged black and white photos of men and women. The frames were of gold leaf, and the overhead chandeliers made them almost glow. Below each, a gold plaque listed the names with their odd titles. Some of them stood out. *Master Guide Thomas Anderson, Skilled Perceptive Samuel Cogelow.*

"I've seen those titles on names before," Sarah said, "in books that Emmie and I ran across recently."

Alex nodded. "They trained with Old Man Lennox Temper and his son when they were connected with Carey Kali. Have you heard of them?"

Sarah tilted her head. "No, not really."

"It's one of the original charters; Temper House started there but branched off. Old Man Temper's vision didn't align with Carey Kali, just as others didn't, so he took that vision and made it a reality. He built this place to help train psychics, hone their skills. What my parents stood for, worked so hard for, was important." He gave her a shy smile. "*Is* important, I guess. I hope I can help you."

Alex continued leading her to the back of the house. An open door revealed an extensive library with a massive table centered beneath soft, modern lights and tall windows that looked out over the backyard. She recognized the view and glanced toward the ceiling. Her room was directly above them.

They passed a study that had antiques but looked freshly painted, with updated windows and plenty of modern comforts like a computer desk, an upholstered armchair, a small sofa, and hand-carved wooden sculptures of several animals in one corner. A plush oval rug covered most of the wood floor.

"You don't do Christmas?" she asked. She hadn't seen a single decoration, and they were less than three weeks away from it.

"We're not big on it, no," Alex said. "Atheist parents."

"Yes, but—"

"I mean very atheist," he clarified. "As in, no way. Do you like it? I'm sorry if you'll miss all the fun and excitement leading to it."

"Oh, no, no. I can do without it sometimes. It's just nice with the snow and all."

"May the gods have mercy on our souls if it ever snows in St. Augustine."

They both laughed.

Passing the last door, which was closed, Alex gestured to it. "We keep this room reserved especially for Cecilia. Her own private meditation room. You can see the garden and the zoo best from in there—she has the largest windows—but she's in there now, and I don't want to disturb her."

"I've met her. Just briefly."

A pained smile crossed his face. "Was she singing? She is really the sweetest person you've ever met."

Sarah nodded sympathetically as his sorrow radiated through her. The poor man, he felt for everyone.

He turned toward the dining room. "But let's get you fed. I'm sure you're starving by now."

Alex seated Sarah at the table, pushing in her chair, and brought in the final food items from the kitchen before leading Cecilia out by the arm from the room they had just passed minutes earlier. He sat beside Sarah while assisting Cecilia with her food on his other side. The young woman's blonde hair was neatly parted off to one side, with soft flowing layers obscuring one eye and the shorter side pulled back in a clip. Her pastel pink floral dress covered her shoulders with a modest v-neck in the front. An elegant, yet warm look that defied the December weather. Almost on cue, Lorelei joined them as soon as everything was ready and sat directly across from Sarah.

When the woman reached out for a plate of food, Sarah spotted a bandage across Lorelei's forearm that she hadn't noticed before. Sarah hesitated to say anything about it, but she sensed a strange heat emanating from it and her nursing instincts took over. "Did you hurt yourself? I'd be happy to take a look at it."

Alex followed Sarah's gaze, and his smile at his sister seemed somewhat wry. "Will you let her, Lorelei?"

Lorelei put her arm under the table. "It's just a cut. A rare moment of carelessness."

Alex took great care to make sure that Sarah had everything she needed, moving each dish closer to her plate and offering to fill her cup with water or a drink. But he was even more attentive to Cecilia, cutting the vegetables into small pieces and making sure she could manage her food.

Lorelei laughed and spoke to Alex. "It's embarrassing to watch you."

"Then don't watch," Alex said.

Lorelei turned to Sarah. "Such a good, traditional boy, isn't he? Honoring his mom and dad today."

"It's an anniversary," Sarah said.

"At least you honor them on one day." Lorelei pretended to clap.

Alex stared at the dishes of food on the table. "They taught me everything I know. Their blood still runs in my veins."

"So people say. The dead live on in us." Lorelei gestured to Cecilia with a shocked face. "Isn't that her day dress? Why didn't you ask her if she wanted to dress up for the anniversary party?"

Cecilia's voice rose between them, "One little duck went out one day..." She turned her face toward the window and continued in a mumble, "Over the hill and far away... Mother duck said, Quack, quack, quack, quack... no little ducks came back."

Alex explained to Sarah, "Cecilia had a sort of stroke last year."

"A sort," Lorelei mocked.

Sarah looked from one sibling to the other as if watching a boxing fight throughout the meal. Alex had warned her about the situation and her embarrassment kept her lips tightly closed, but she was already getting used to the strangeness. Didn't all siblings fight like they wanted to kill each other and then play like best friends the next moment? The animosity between them was palpable, although the reasons for it still weren't clear. Maybe Lorelei didn't think Alex honored the parents enough, or maybe she resented him because he hadn't kept the school going. Yet the woman hadn't exactly welcomed Sarah, his student, with open arms when Alex brought her in.

When they were done eating, Alex excused himself first. "I need to take Cecilia upstairs, as she always likes me to be there when she falls asleep."

"Isn't he sweet? Always there for her." Lorelei smiled. "He's going to brush her hair and all. So cute." She got up abruptly, threw down her napkin and told Sarah, "You can leave it all there; Alex loves to clean up. He doesn't sleep half the night, so it gives him something to do."

Sarah looked to Alex for a reaction, but he was already busy with Cecilia. Standing and following Alex and Cecilia, Sarah paused at the bottom of the stairs, watching him stroke his sister's hair as he encouraged her every step.

Sarah couldn't stay quiet another moment. "I can help."

Alex shook his head. "I'm afraid a stranger's contact might upset her. You understand."

Sarah's nod went unnoticed.

At the top of the stairs, Alex turned back to Sarah. "We'll start our training in the morning. I hope you have a good night."

As they walked away, Cecilia's soft voice echoed the same rhyme from earlier. "One little duck went out one day... Over the hill and far away... Mother duck said, Quack, quack, quack, quack... no little ducks came back."

❧ 1 3 ❧

Sarah's grandmother sat at the edge of the bed stroking Sarah's hair as her soothing voice repeated the words of the children's song over and over.

"Little Bo Peep has lost her sheep..."

The morning light beamed across the room, across her grandmother's face that smiled down lovingly at her. Her eyes were so full of hope, and Sarah didn't want to disappoint her, but there was something Sarah had to do. Something very important. Something that terrified her.

Her grandmother became her strength in that moment as she tried to recharge her courage to face the difficulties that lay ahead.

"I haven't faced anything like this before, Grandma Beth," Sarah said. "Everything is so strange. What would you do?"

"You're stronger than any person I've known. You know the answer."

"But I don't—"

Her grandmother started singing again, brushing Sarah's cheeks and gently pushing her hair away from her face in long, steady strokes. The old woman's warm touch swept away some of that fear that paralyzed her now as she lay in bed with the bright afternoon sunlight streaming in through an open window beside them.

Sarah focused on her grandmother's caresses. "I wish I could stay like this forever."

Grandma Beth pulled her hand away. "But what about Little Bo Peep?"

Sarah met her grandmother's stern gaze. "What?"

"She lost her sheep," the woman said, as if correcting her, "and she didn't know where to find them."

"That's just a children's rhyme, Grandma."

"No!"

The sun fell below the horizon and darkness swept around them, thick with swirling dark gray clouds. The warmth left the room and Sarah stared into her grandmother's agitated face.

"What's going on, Grandma Beth?" Sarah's heart raced faster. "I'm scared."

Her grandmother spoke more loudly. "Little Bo Peep lost her sheep. Little Bo Peep lost her sheep."

The rhyme echoed through Sarah's mind. "I need to wake up."

Her grandmother shook her head, her eyes full of anger now, saying the lines over and over like a reprimand.

Sarah conceded and echoed the words. "Little Bo Peep..."

"... has lost her sheep!" Her grandmother's face lit up. "... And doesn't know where to find them! Leave them alone and they will come home... wagging their tails behind them!"

Her grandmother laughed and clapped her hands, then watched with wide eyes as Sarah repeated the lines again.

The old woman spoke the lines faster, again and again, clapping her hands as Sarah tried to keep up with the odd behavior. The words flowed faster and faster until they jumbled together in a mess of slurred speech until she stopped suddenly, and the room went dark.

Within the darkness, a loud clap jarred her from her sleep.

Sarah awoke suddenly. Her eyes snapped open, and Cecilia

was sitting on the edge of her bed clapping her one good hand against the back of the curled one.

"What—" Sarah shuddered. "What are you doing here?"

Cecilia's eyes were wide, and a bright smile stretched across her face as she clapped again in a fluctuating tempo.

"Little Bo Peep has lost her sheep...
And doesn't know where to find them.
Leave them alone and they'll come home,
Bringing their tails behind them."

She spoke "Leave them alone" with emphasis.

Sarah shifted beneath her covers, inching away from Cecilia's encroaching presence. "Are you lost?"

Cecilia stared back with a confused gaze and said the line again while watching Sarah's reaction.

Sarah looked at the window. It was dark outside. She guessed she hadn't slept for more than an hour, judging by her exhaustion. "I'm sorry, Cecilia." Sarah sat up. "It's too late for games."

Cecilia scowled.

Sarah spoke softly. "Is that a song you sang as a child?"

The young woman didn't answer but repeated it a little louder.

Sarah watched Cecilia's expression hover between giddy anticipation and devastated frustration. Sarah completed the rhyme. "... And doesn't know where to find them."

Cecilia struggled to her feet and clapped a few more times before while steadying herself against the bed.

"But neither of us should be awake at this hour." Sarah slipped her feet out from under the covers and stood beside Cecilia, reaching gently toward her arm. "Let's get you back to your own room. We both need sleep."

Sarah's nursing mode kicked into high gear. Cecilia was so much like any other patient she had encountered at the hospital with dementia or confusion. And Cecilia didn't resist. The young woman even held out her arm as if she understood what Sarah intended to do.

Sarah guided Cecilia back to her room. The hallways echoed their footsteps, and she shivered in the cool night air.

Was it normal for Cecilia to wander the hallways at night? Sarah supposed that the allure of a new guest in the house had drawn Cecilia out of her room, and maybe it had never happened before, but she would need to mention it to Alex the next day. It wasn't safe, in any case.

Sarah guided Cecilia into the young woman's room, leaving the lights off to spare her own tired eyes and allowing the moon spilling in through the shaded windows to light the way. Large photos of Cecilia hung on one wall and again showed the young woman before the "accident" that Alex had mentioned. Cecilia's expression in the photos was the epitome of joy as she fed the animals, even embracing them.

She cared for them. Probably grew up with them.

A four-poster bed filled one side of the room to the right, decorated with white and pink laced bedding and several plush pillows. Cecilia had pushed the bedding to the side, no doubt when she'd escaped to Sarah's room earlier.

Sarah helped Cecilia get into bed. "No more adventures tonight."

Cecilia gave no indication that she understood, but turned over on her side and faced the window with her eyes wide open.

Sarah followed Cecilia's gaze and stepped over to the window, pushing aside the blinds and staring out into the darkness of the backyard toward the zoo. There were still some faint lights along the main path leading toward a pavilion.

A lone shadow caught her attention, a figure walking away from the house. The person's gait and outline were clear. Alex.

A flurry of questions flashed through her mind. Wasn't it a bit late to take a walk in the zoo? Had one of the animals gotten sick or needed help? Lorelei had said Alex stayed up half the night, but what was in the pavilion? More animals?

As she wondered, something thumped against the window only inches from her face. She jumped back, letting the blinds crack against the glass, but she returned a moment later and peeked out again. A fluttering shape appeared in the faint light. A bird had somehow gotten drawn to the window and was desperately trying to get in. She guessed it was a pigeon, judging by the gray feathers and size, but after it fluttered, swooped and landed near the base of the window, she caught sight of its full body and gasped. Its feathers were ruffled, as if it had just escaped a vicious attack on its life, and its head was tilted to one side with one eye socket empty.

Sarah's heart went out to it. *Poor thing. Has it gotten into a fight with another animal?*

It seemed to stare at her for a moment before fluttering up into the air. It hovered and swooped in a circle before it came crashing back down. Its beak cracked against the glass as if it had done it on purpose, as if trying to break through.

Sarah stumbled away from the window, holding up her hands over her face.

"Leave them alone, and they'll come home..." Cecilia mumbled from her bed.

❧ 14 ❧

Finn floated in the water with his face above the surface, the sun and air touching his skin as the waves gently rocked him. He had chosen a quiet section of beach, hundreds of yards away from the nearest person, and the silence truly was golden.

The ocean was alive beneath him. Schools of tropical fish, corals and sea turtles had swum by, sometimes approaching so close he could have reached down and touched them within the depths of the glassy water. Even the threat of encountering an ocean predator didn't scare him now. A local had warned him to beware of stingrays and not to try petting the nurse sharks or get too close to the barracuda. Finn knew but thanked the man anyway. But nobody had warned him about the biggest threat in the area. A bold woman with wandering eyes and hands.

And she had used some sort of drug to make him see things. She was like freaking Don Juan in the Castañeda books, trying to open the doors to his consciousness.

Although he had experimented with some drugs in college, like most of his peers, he avoided them now at all costs. And the idea of thrusting them on others unknowingly was especially detestable, even if they were leaves, or "natural stuff," as the witch would say.

And yet... he couldn't rid his mind of her face as he'd insulted and pushed her. She must be a resilient woman, but she was also generous and giving. She *had* been trying to help him, that much he knew. It wasn't her fault she didn't know his trauma with drugs—that his brother had probably died because of them.

Didn't he just have a wonderful way of being horrible?

He swam back to the shore without putting in much effort, slowing at moments when he turned on his back to watch the clouds pass overhead. The palm trees rustled along the beach in the light breeze as his feet touched the sandy shoreline and he wiped away the water from his eyes.

Someone was waiting for him. She was sitting on his towel, watching him as he made his way toward her. Natalia.

He met her gaze, and she pulled another clean towel from his bag, handing it to him without speaking when he arrived beside her. Wiping the dripping seawater from his hair and chest, he stood staring out across the water before dropping beside her and throwing the towel around his back and shoulders. "I'm sorry."

"I think it was a perfect example of why you came in the first place. You turned nasty in ten seconds."

He bowed his head. "Too nasty."

"*Órale* is Mexican, by the way."

"I know."

"So you said it on purpose to put all the latinos together like they are the same."

"You called me gringo. And I don't think things like that..."

"You think them. They go through your head, even as a man of culture, as they do through everyone else's throughout life's unending frustrations, though you're not aware of it. As I told you. You know it's a way to hurt or dismiss me—and you desperately wanted to do that."

He met her gaze. "Natalia, you drugged me without my consent."

Her voice strained. "You come here thinking you want to

heal or find yourself, and then you close yourself off, protect yourself as if you were in a war." She smiled. "Lucky for you that I'm used to it."

"I don't like that I turned nasty on you, but I don't like to do drugs without knowing either."

"So many opinions..." She looked at him. "I'd still like to talk."

He nodded.

"Good. So tell me, you saw two people in the liquid and smoke..."

He looked down. "Yes."

"One, the girl you love."

He closed his eyes for a moment, picturing Sarah's beaming smile *before* the ordeal at Whisper House. Natalia made the relationship sound so simple.

"The woman you don't deserve," she added.

His body tensed as he let out a quick, sarcastic laugh. Now *there* was a bit of truth.

"And the other one you saw?" Natalia asked. "Who was that?"

"My brother, Neil."

"He died?"

It took him a moment to say, "Suicide. Shot himself in my parents' basement."

"Ah! Survivor's guilt."

Finn clenched his teeth. *So now the New Age empress is a psychologist as well. What's the diagnosis, Dr. Natalia? It's nothing I couldn't find after a quick Google search.*

She touched his forearm as if to calm him, and he flinched, although her touch was gentle. From the corner of his eye, he saw that she wasn't looking at him. She wasn't reaching to flirt with him this time. As a wave of peace swept over him, he let out a long slow breath, and the stress of the moment also dissipated.

"Let's start again," she said.

He opened his mouth to speak but a sudden gust of wind ran

across his face almost as if to silence his voice for a moment, and he closed it again.

"A sibling is closer to us than anyone, even more so than parents or children," Natalia said. "It's not just the DNA, but growing up together, learning together, becoming together. Even if you fight, it's like that. To lose a sibling truly is like having a part of us ripped away. So it's one of the hardest things, which is why you turned your grief into anger. That's much easier to bear. Tell me, do you often put yourself in harm's way?"

A thousand reckless moments flashed through his mind. *Relentlessly reckless Finn...*

She continued, "Do you often behave in ways you know you shouldn't?"

The vividly awful moments just kept coming. So many times he had risked the loss of life and limb or simply done what was stupid while knowing it... He had hurt others too, in what he said, and through his absence and contempt.

He met her gaze for a moment, then looked away. "All right, you got me. I suppose I want to hurt myself because my brother went away and I stayed. Fair enough. But now I've got others with me, and I don't want to hurt them. That's the point. They're good people, do you understand? The best. I absolutely can't risk hurting them anymore."

"I understand. But you've got to see then that you cannot continue to hurt yourself. If you wish for your own harm, it reaches anyone close to you. If you wish for your own harm, the bad spirits find you and play with you. You understand?"

He laughed. "Right. As if that's so easy to fix. Thirty years of therapy coming up."

"No." She smiled and shook her head. "I'm here for you. That's the whole point of Jason sending you. You need to believe, though, and you're short on belief. You've seen things and you still doubt and doubt because you're protecting yourself in the wrong way. The protection is what hurts you."

He turned and faced her. She did the same, and moved in

even closer so that her knees touched him a little. As he tried to articulate the emotions welling up in his chest, the sun slipped behind a cloud and the temperature dropped noticeably across his skin.

She reached out and took his face in her hands. Her eyes and her smile were like an embrace, making him warm even in the sudden shade.

"Help me," he said, "if you can. I really need you to."

"Yes, I can, but you need to stop your judgment. I'm not drugging you, as you say. Not really. Not only."

He thought about it. "Is it the only way?"

"It's *my* way."

He nodded. "All right. What else?"

"You must do what you fear the most."

"What is that?"

"Show me your pain."

Sarah's horrified face from Whisper House filled his mind. "I will," he said. "But just make sure of one thing, that nobody, *nothing*, can ever get to me again."

15

"How well do you know this guy?" Emmie asked. Jason's attention was locked on the heavy New Orleans traffic that raced around them, but he looked at her a moment later, probably sensing her anxiety because he had that "Relax, everything's good" message in his eyes.

"For years. I've met him or called him whenever I needed scholarly advice," he said. "He's an expert on artifacts, knows more about the historical aspects of the psychic world than anyone I've ever met. Museums and collectors around the world hire him out by the hour to do appraisals, so he's a great resource for someone like me." He gestured from him to her. "And now us."

"Another occult nerd," Emmie said with a brief laugh. "But can we trust him? I mean, the way Dr. Albright died means someone from the psychic world really had it in for him."

"Howard has no powers. It can't have been him, which is why I'm sure he's safe."

Emmie nodded once and stared out the window as they passed through an older section of the city. Jason slowed down as a streetcar track appeared in front of them and crossed it slowly, as if feeling sorry for the rented car.

The phone's GPS showed their destination only a short distance away. After escaping the crowded city streets, they moved silently into a residential area and Jason gestured ahead. "Almost there."

Within a few blocks, Jason recognized a two-story home and parked, shutting off the engine. The house was hidden behind a thick, sprawling tree and a row of hedges running parallel with the sidewalk, but she could still see the structure's clean, minimalistic lines and all the glass that surrounded it.

Before leaving the car, Jason turned to Emmie with a somber expression. "Just some advice before we go in. Despite everything I said a moment ago about trusting this guy, better let me do the talking, okay?"

"Trying to silence a woman?" she asked with a smirk.

"Cancel me later," he joked. "Right now, we'll need diplomacy and that's not exactly where you shine. Unlike in just about every other—"

"You don't have to lay it on that thick."

They jokingly narrowed eyes at each other and got out of the car, stepping toward the home's front entrance. Leaning closer to her, Jason spoke under his breath. "He likes to learn things at every opportunity, so it's probably better not to tell him about your psychic gift at all."

Emmie eyed him. "Deaf and dumb too. Would that help?"

Jason grinned. "*There's* that feisty spirit I find so irresistible." He kissed her on the cheek.

They stopped at the front door and Jason pushed a glowing button to activate the video doorbell.

Howard answered breathlessly, as if he'd hurried to answer it. "That you, Jason?"

"It is, my friend."

A moment later, the door's latch electronically clicked open and they stepped inside.

Howard appeared from around the corner ahead. He was a heavyset man in his sixties with gray hair and round glasses, but he moved quickly toward them, welcoming Jason with a bear hug and a side-eyed glance at Emmie. "Who is this?"

"Just Emmie." Jason gestured to her.

"Hello, Just-Emmie," Howard said wryly, and invited her in after Jason. "Where have you been, Jason? I tried contacting you a few weeks ago. You never answered me."

"I must have missed the message."

"I sent three. You're ignoring me?"

"Absolutely not. Just had a few rough weeks."

Howard let it go and led them into the living room area. It was just as minimalistic as the outside, with blinding white walls and mid-century design furniture. Except for the occasional odd artifact and macabre painting, nothing much gave away the man's association with the occult.

Howard took a seat in a recliner and motioned to the leather couch across from him. He eyed them both before clapping his hands together. "All right. You had something you wanted me to see?"

Jason gestured to Emmie. "On her phone."

Emmie understood and brought up the photo she'd taken at Dr. Albright's apartment. She handed her phone to Howard before sitting on the couch next to Jason.

"Just the one photo?"

"Just that," Jason said. "There's a symbol. Do you see it?"

Howard nodded and said somewhat solemnly, "Dr. Albright did deal in symbols. I'll say that for him."

His eyes became a bit lost, as if he were thinking about the dead professor or afraid to look at the image they had.

"What do you make of the symbol in the photo?" Jason leaned toward Howard, gesturing at the phone. "Zoom into the chair. There's a symbol burnt there."

Adjusting his glasses, Howard did. Then he stared at the symbol, and his expression changed to shock. "A rose," he mumbled. "They dared..."

Emmie and Jason waited for Howard to finish his thought,

which never happened. Instead, the man stood abruptly. "I'm afraid I can't help you."

Meeting Jason's gaze, Emmie saw he looked as confused as she was.

Howard's hands clenched into fists, then frowned while turning toward the door as if to usher them out.

"That's it?" Jason asked.

"I'm sorry." Howard started walking and didn't look back.

"We can pay for your expertise, if that's what you mean."

"No, that's not what I mean. You need to leave." Howard opened the door wide and stood beside it. "Jason, I'm serious."

"We must have hit a nerve," Jason asked as he walked to the door with Emmie. "Why won't you tell us the significance of the rose?"

"Because I suggest you both go home and forget about it."

Emmie stopped and faced Howard. "You know exactly what it is. Why is it dangerous?"

"I know who you are, Just-Emmie. Do you think I move in this world and don't know about your parents? About your potential squandered away in some backwater town?"

"Backwater town?" Emmie's body tensed, and she bristled on the edge of losing her cool. "Listen—"

Jason took her arm and stepped forward. "Why the sudden attitude? Dr. Albright was murdered and if you have information—"

"This is not for amateurs. Certainly not for two psychics who failed to complete their training years ago." His gaze moved from Emmie to Jason. "You're in way over your head, so don't bother running around like you can solve this, messing with the big stuff. Neither of you has what it takes to see this thing through."

"Then help us understand," Jason said.

Howard scowled. "You've probably already complicated things by getting into the doctor's home before the others had a chance to investigate. Read my lips, Jason: This isn't something you can handle."

"We've handled more in the last few months than you've probably done in a lifetime." Emmie's face warmed.

Howard rubbed his forehead as his face turned red. "You can't possibly understand. This kind of power corrupts even the best of us, even you, and it's the responsibility of people like Albright to make sure things like this don't happen, and now he's gone. Others will take his place—it's an efficient organization. You should explain this to her, Jason."

Jason pulled Emmie to him. "I've underestimated how much you know, Howard."

"Yes, you've underestimated *everything*," he answered.

Emmie stepped outside with Jason's arm around her shoulders as Howard let out an exasperated sigh and stood in the doorway behind them. She wanted to turn back and scream at Howard to just *tell them*, but it was pointless to argue, wasn't it? A man like Howard wasn't about to give up control to *two failed psychics*.

"You can't stop us," she said anyway. She was sick of being warned away from *things*.

"No, I can't, and I won't. But there is an order to things. And it should never be messed with."

16

A lex brought Sarah to the library. Sitting her at the oval table in the center of the room, he retrieved from a long, flat drawer several old tintype etchings, handling them as if they were newborns and placing them carefully in front of Sarah. One showed a woman in a white dress with outstretched arms with beams of light coming out of her. Before her was an idyllic country scene, with trees and hills; behind her, a darker scene with starlike bursts of light. A world of life, and a world of death, clearly, and she between them. Something resembling souls passed through her to become the starbursts. Just as they had passed through Sarah.

The hair on the back of her neck bristled.

"This is what I think you may be." He tapped his finger on the words below the etching, written in bold type: THE DOOR OF LIGHT.

As she stared with fascination at the image, Alex eagerly brought an oversized leather-bound volume to the table, which shook as he placed it down. Opening the cover, he passed the pages to her with care. It was an old book that had similar illustrations and old-fashioned printing underneath them. The text was in medieval English—or something like it—and it was hard to tell "s" from "f," which slowed her understanding of its meaning. Alex began following the words with his finger as he read, somewhat translating for her.

"The bearer of such a gift has power beyond knowing... The door of light shall not come in numbers but in heaven-sent mission..."

"What does it mean?" she asked.

"That you are very, very special."

"If it is me..." she mumbled.

"Yes. And that it's a very healing power. *Extreme* healing."

"Do you really think I am it?"

"We'll try to find out." He sat down across from her and met her gaze. He tapped the book, whose title was *Of Nature and Means,* and added, "The texts talk about channeling the energy around you to shine and alter the physical vibrations of matter, transforming disturbances back into alignment with the universal blueprint for all living things."

"Oh, God," she groaned. "It sounds like something an old ghost was talking about in the last haunted house we visited. Driving everyone crazy with it."

"Theory does that sometimes," Alex said with a small laugh. "And the intellect can get in the way of skills. But it basically means that if it is you, not only *can* you do it, but you have a *responsibility* to develop it. For the sake of the world."

"The heaven-sent mission bit?" She contorted her face. "Sounds a bit much?"

"I don't believe so. It's obviously a power so rare and beautiful that you have a chance to change life itself."

She skimmed through some of the text again, then glanced up at him wryly. "Let me ask this. Can it heal broken hearts?"

He nodded once. "It can heal *anything.*"

Finn's broken spirit flashed through her mind again. He had been broken for so long. If all of this was true, she could truly help others to an extent she'd never imagined. She met Alex's gaze—she could wipe away so much pain. It was all she'd ever wanted to do.

"When do we start?" she asked.

He closed the book in her hands and nodded. "Right now. I'll make copies of some pages for you to read this evening. Consider it your homework. We should start with some practical training first."

Alex led her out into the backyard toward the garden beside the zoo. The stone path to the garden running beside the zoo was no more than a few feet across, and some overgrown trees threatened to block their way at times as they walked beside each other in silence. The pleasant smell of flowers and cool air was refreshing, and she couldn't help but feel a little guilty basking in that slice of paradise as her friends in Minnesota froze.

Sarah continued walking toward the garden but stopped suddenly. A face peered out from within the darkness of the live oaks and vegetation several yards on her right. The face was of a white and angelic child kneeling in prayer. The details of the form became clearer as she stared at it. A marble statue.

Alex gestured to the statue. "You'll find dozens of graves and monuments back here, some dating back to the years after Old Man Temper founded the house. But as I mentioned before, you won't find any ghosts here. People died *naturally*... Despite the age of the house, it remains spirit-free. If there were any spirits still lingering within its walls, I'm sure one of the psychics who trained here would have intervened by now."

Sarah eyed the tall grass at the edge of the property. "I'm not worried about ghosts."

Pushing through the overgrown pathway with both hands, they came out into a large circular clearing lined with flowers and tall plants in every direction. Everything was meticulously arranged, with the flowerbeds curated to showcase the unique beauty of each flower species. The sweet fragrance was intoxicating. Sarah took in a deep breath.

Stone paths paralleled long rows of red and yellow tulips, white daisies, purple azaleas, pink lilies, camellias, and a rainbow of roses. Taller green plants accented the colors beside a running water fountain that stood at the end of a narrow stream running down the center. Bees and butterflies flitted from flower to flower, creating an atmosphere of peace and tranquility. An oasis from the chaos of the outside world.

Alex gestured to somewhere within the maze of flowers ahead. "We're going to sit right in the middle of it. You'll draw your strength from living but non-sentient things at first, such as plants and flowers. They have light too."

"I know..." Sarah said. She and Emmie had practiced with that, an easy exercise for amateurs according to Betty's books, so she hoped for more challenging tasks from Alex ahead.

Staying close to her side, Alex led her around the sprawling rows of flowers and plants, weaving between the hedges that separated the various sections of a larger mosaic, and they sat in a small patch of grass that was oddly different from the Minnesota grass.

They faced each other, and after she had gotten comfortable, he took her hands and looked into her eyes. Her stomach fluttered with anxiety as she waited for instructions. But the silence between them dragged on for what seemed like forever until he finally closed his eyes. She did the same, although peeking out a few times until she accepted the awkward moment and relaxed.

After a couple of minutes, he said, "The first step is for you to become aware of the life in the area more acutely than you have ever been before. As an empath, you'll feel the light of all this life and absorb it, letting it become energy and power in you."

Sarah nodded with her eyes still closed. How hard could it be?

She focused on the plants around her. The roses, the live oaks, the grass, the weeds, the palm trees. No emotions from them, but she could still feel a soft radiance emanating from each in her mind. Collectively, their light created a vibrant landscape of colors so overwhelming she could almost see them. They were alive—or life itself—and their energy was different from the one humans emitted, but still had the same elemental essence of spirit.

"Can you see them?" Alex asked.

"I do."

"Try to draw in some of their light. Bask in it like you would when turning your face toward the sun."

She did just that, allowing the radiation of a single rose to pass through her while almost merging with it. But as she swept within its energy, absorbing the transcendental moment, the shifting waves overlapped and then parted, revealing that she had affected its frequencies. It seemed to wilt even as she moved and shared the same space for a moment, blending her energy with the rose's to produce a strange new mixture of light between them. She wasn't possessing the flower—not for a moment—yet they formed a symbiotic relationship as their energies danced.

But the longer she played, the more its light dissipated. Stripped of its life force for only a short time, the rose succumbed to a darkness that formed and surrounded it. The flower shriveled as its light faded.

"I disrupted its light." A bit of sadness swept through Sarah. "I think I'm killing it."

"Don't hold back. See if you can replenish its energy."

It *was* just a flower, after all.

She moved through the flower again, drawing in as much warmth as she could, and this time it reacted as if it had become an extension of her own body. The delicate connection bristled between them. She had weakened it, but her light passed through it again like an invisible hand, and it was clear she could do more than just share its space. She could push its energy back inside its form like a sculptor, drawing it from an unseen source beyond her perception.

Within a minute, she had restored it to its original condition. She opened her eyes.

"You got it." Alex nodded with a wide smile. "And we move right on, now that you're full of energy. What we need to do now is to roam. If you allow your senses, which have absorbed all this light, to search, you'll feel the emotions around the place. I want you to let that happen as if you were a device looking for a signal. Like when all the Wi-Fi spots start appearing on your phone, every spot that's around. You are just increasing your range. But first, come through me. You are used to my energy, and I know how to roam. Use me to strengthen your signal."

She smiled at the analogy. Alex must have seen that the medieval stuff wasn't her forte, but she could readily understand what he meant now.

Sarah did as he said, first finding his signal, which she already knew and trusted. Her energy took something of a piggy back ride on his as he showed her the spirits around them. She was floating on his wave, and he was guiding her, making her aware of not only the other psychics in the house—the sisters—but also the groundskeeper and the animals nearby. The human emotions faded in and out as she moved past Alex to rely on her own focus, direct it both near and far. Some emotions burned like a raging fire, while others escaped and hid, and still others were cold and bitter.

"It touches you a great deal, doesn't it?" Alex's voice sounded as if it were inside her head, just as it had done when they had spoken long distance to each other. "The way others feel."

Still holding her hands, he had let his spirit retreat, like an adult who allows a child to go off on a bicycle or skate while staying behind to watch, ready to jump in as needed. He had given her the first push and now let her roam freely.

"Yes," she answered.

"Some spirits don't respond to your help, but you can hone your skills with their energy. It's like using a whetstone to sharpen a sword. Even an enemy spirit can become your tool."

"There's so many spirits."

"You can get close to them, but don't cross the line."

"What line?"

"A barrier surrounding human spirits. Think of it as their personal space. Don't invade that sphere. Some might be stronger than you."

Like Lorelei, she supposed. Even Cecilia might be stronger and try to draw Sarah into the woman's feeble mind.

"I sense animals too. Birds are nearby. I can tell by the way their hearts palpitate."

"Perfect."

"I sense something... so strange. Like... old?"

He laughed. "I think it's an alligator."

Her eyes would have flown open, but he squeezed her hands reassuringly.

"Let's pick one of those, just to make it interesting."

"One of the alligators?"

"Exactly."

"Oh, yuck."

"Shhh. No judgment. You can learn from anything."

She focused on the alligator. "It's not... not like a spirit. More like—"

"It's pure instinct," Alex said in a low, hypnotic voice, as if he too could feel it and had felt it. "Do you get anything else from it?"

Again, she slowly relaxed, but the sensation of meeting an animal jarred her concentration. "Am I trying to read its mind?"

"It doesn't have one like we do, just—"

"Instinct," she said.

"You can go into it. There's no danger here."

"I should invade the barrier?"

"Go on."

And she let herself go. Her light invaded that darkness.

"Don't grab it," Alex said. "Don't let it invade you. Be in it."

It was like dwelling in a cave, wanting to run out to the air again, but she persisted until repulsion started giving way to something else. A strange blending. This thing didn't think, didn't feel, had no emotions. It knew. It was perfect as it was.

The thing had incredible strength, and it had been like that for a long, long, long time.

She began to draw strength from it. Knowledge. She could not leave anything to it, but she could take from it.

Something surged in her chest and head. The creature's awareness flared in a panic and instinctively struck back against the intrusion, catching her off guard. She opened her eyes with a gasp.

Alex opened his more slowly. "Tell me," he said after a moment.

"It was... so strange. I was disgusted, and then—I was learning."

"A lot of things might surprise you over the next few days."

"Am I going to become an alligator-woman or something?"

His laugh was like a boy's. "Definitely not. But if your teeth start growing, I'll let you know."

"Seriously, Alex," she held on to his hands. "Sharing like this, with any spirit. Isn't it dangerous?"

He smiled gently. "That's why I'm here."

"I've given myself over to a spirit before, during automatic writings," she said. "I guess I learned to control them so they don't take over."

"That's good."

She couldn't help thinking that it was a pity he'd decided not to keep teaching. She appreciated his patience and encouragement, qualities that would've made him an excellent mentor. He made her feel safe.

"We're done for today," he said.

As they walked back to the house, he touched her shoulder. "You should take a nap. You'll need to replenish your energy, or we can't advance to the next level."

She *did* feel drained but had rarely taken a nap, but she kept that to herself. Yet when she got to her room and dropped herself into bed without undressing, she found herself startled out of a deep sleep an hour later with Alex telling her through the closed door that it was dinnertime.

Dinner that evening was more pleasant too. Maybe it was the nap, or maybe it was that Lorelei was absent at the table, but she *did* feel energized as they shared a few light-hearted stories of their youth. Alex showed the same care toward Cecelia as he always seemed to, and they each went their separate ways without drama.

The next day, they worked through many of the same methods, but with Sarah able to ride out and find the "signals" of life on her own from the start. Alex's presence was again in the background and yet protective as she encountered the lifeforms in the zoo and beyond, feeling the individuality of each entity.

Another nap, and another dinner without Lorelei. Sarah knew—felt—the oldest sibling was moving around the house as if to avoid any contact with her. Not that she minded.

On the third day, Alex said something different.

"This morning you'll need to try to find something that may not be well."

"Not well? Some hurt animal? How will I know?"

"You're a nurse. Reach out and find a creature that's suffering."

They went back into meditative mode, and she started to listen. To feel. She might even be swaying as she sat there and turned her face one way and another until it was almost as if a knife had slashed the air in front of her. A heartbeat that spiked and slowed. She found it: a bird. She felt its pain as it struggled in search of food—so hungry. It couldn't move normally. Oh, its wing was injured, and she had a sudden knowledge of how it had occurred. The alligator—the same one she had connected with—had failed to take it down but had harmed it enough to prevent the bird from escaping by flight. The bird moved restlessly through the water, searching for food, but it also was resigned to its fate.

"A bird is injured," she said softly, "and it knows it's going to die."

"You see the world through its eyes..."

It was a statement, as Alex was there with her. She realized that she was seeing the details of the swamp through the bird's eyes. Its pain became her own.

Dangerous to feel it.

Had the thought come from her or Alex?

"Envelop it with your light," Alex told her softly. "The same light you created at the house you mentioned to attract the spirits. You may not succeed this time, but we can try."

There wasn't the same urgency that she'd felt at Whisper House to create that light. Back then, her emotions had been so overwhelmed by everything that had happened, and the pressure had given her focus and certainty. But she still recognized the essence of what she needed to produce. Taking that spark of light, she focused it and made it grow almost as if life itself were manifesting in that energy. The feathers and flesh and skin became her consciousness, and the blueprints were there within her intuition.

"Think of your studies," Alex said inside her head. "Think of what you would see in a microscope. The small parts that make up this life."

Sarah went back to her biology classes and saw its cells; she had to shift the energy to that tiny level, building the bird back to its original design.

The bird didn't resist as she held its life in her spirit-hands; it was on the brink of moving on or living fully in physical form.

The alligator was nearby, moving closer since its hunger had driven it to find the bird again. It wasn't so far that she could prevent it from capturing its prey before she was done.

She hurried. The bird's pain faded, and as it fluttered to fly away, she held it back to complete what she had started. "Almost done."

The warmth flowed from her through the bird as the alligator moved within feet of capturing it.

Fusing the last of its cells, she let it go. The sound of fluttering wings and chirps came from beyond the garden to her right as the bird shot off into the air. She exhaled and dropped her head forward. "I think I did it."

Alex's gaze followed the soaring bird. "You did it." He leaned forward, still holding Sarah's hand. The elation in his voice was contagious. "You were shining more than the sun!"

"Was there light?" she asked. "I couldn't feel it, I was so focused on—"

"I think you're it," he whispered, as if talking to himself. "Yes, I think you are."

He seemed so moved for her, so genuine in his joy, that she leaned forward and embraced him. He put his face against her shoulder and let her hold him for a long moment.

Yet, despite her success, she was exhausted. Soon he stood and helped her to her feet. As they returned to the house, he steadied her steps with an arm around her shoulder. The interaction had weakened her body as if she had run a marathon.

Before they stepped inside, Lorelei appeared for the first time in three days just inside the doorway. Sarah managed not to jump, though the woman had jarred her. Lorelei clapped her hands as Sarah passed by.

Sarah realized the woman had seen or felt what she had done.

"Enjoying your accomplishment?" Lorelei asked. "You've lit a match, anyway. Let's see if you can start a bonfire."

❧ 17 ❧

Sarah awoke a short time later to a strange sensation flowing through her, as if her bed had touched a low voltage electrical wire. The sensation waved through her whole body and seemed to come from somewhere nearby.

She sat up. Alex had insisted that there were no spirits in the house. No one had died there, anyway, but this was the same familiar intensity she had experienced at the hospital with some dying patients. The intimate, deep sensation wasn't so strong that it caused her great discomfort, but it was impossible to ignore.

She climbed out of bed and went to the door without opening it, feeling the sensation intensify. It was coming from somewhere in the house. She tried to define the feeling—an emotional energy.

Still exhausted from the day's training, she stepped out into the hallway and glanced around. There was a light coming from the end of the hall, past Cecilia's room in the dim, neglected wing of the house. The light seeped out from behind the large double doors she had spotted earlier. Lorelei's area.

Maybe the day's success in healing animals had emboldened

her too much and made her think she could do anything now, but she had to act. The pulse of energy, both seen and felt, lured her forward.

The strength of that feeling wasn't like anything she had encountered before. It had a depth to it, and a hot intensity. She moved past Cecilia's door without stopping. Her footsteps squeaked, even as she moved stealthily ahead.

She imagined Lorelei confronting her in the hallway and how she might respond.

Just checking out a noise. And I'm not sorry.

Moving to the end of the hallway, she passed the last of the renovated light fixtures and stepped into Lorelei's area. The sensation in her chest grew stronger, and she tried to triangulate the source of the intensity luring her as she moved. It was like playing the child's game, Hot and Cold. She was getting warmer now, literally, although she slowed as she walked toward the light radiating from beneath the large double doors. She paused in front of them.

Am I really going in there?

She turned the door handle and opened the door on the right.

The smell of old wood and dust permeated the air as Sarah stepped inside a short corridor; it was like a waiting area with five open doorways, two on her left, two on her right, and one straight ahead at the end. There had been doors over the openings at one time, judging by the worn and splintered door frames, but someone had removed them. The air was chilly, and a slight breeze passed over her face as if someone had turned the air conditioner at full blast. She shivered and covered her arms when the air swept over her skin. Leaving the door open behind her, she felt as if she were walking into a refrigerator.

The glow coming from the doorway straight ahead illuminated the area and spilled into the other rooms. A low buzzing sound helped to mask her footsteps as she moved forward.

At the first doorway, she found that her eyes had adjusted to the darkness. The odd assortment of objects startled her, and they filled every corner and shelf. Cages sat everywhere—hundreds of them, of all sizes and designs, some large enough to hold the largest Saint Bernard, and some smaller ones domed at the top. Surrounding the cages were tables and countertops strewn with hundreds of medical devices, discarded surgical bandages, dressings and adhesives. Empty jars were piled beside them. It appeared that nobody had used most of the equipment in years, except for a few smaller cages near the doorway that sat with doors gaping and white towels padding the tiny floors inside them.

The discovery wasn't surprising. They must have taken care of many animals over the years on the property. Some of them might have been sheltered in that section of the house while ill or recovering. It was a makeshift vet clinic, in a way.

But someone obviously had used the room recently. An open jar of burn ointment and bandage wrappers sat out on the counter next to a sink. Lorelei must have used them to patch her arm when she cut herself.

Moving on to the next doorway, she discovered an assortment of books piled in the corners, mixed with notebooks, some of them propped up beside boxes seemingly sorted and labeled by subject matter. Several old wooden desks and chairs circled the room, all facing in toward the center.

A classroom. Had the previous psychic students studied there? She could almost hear the voice of the instructor guiding them through their lessons.

The two doorways opposite her were also stuffed with abandoned furniture, more books, and boxes stacked without labels. The wallpaper covering one wall was peeling away with some of the wooden structure beneath it exposed. An undisturbed layer of dust lay over everything, with the light glistening off spider webs near the ceiling. It was hard to believe that Lorelei had made that area her home.

She focused again on the streaming light from the last door

at the end of the corridor. Dust particles floated gently in the air, producing a haze that reminded her of the poor air quality she was breathing at that moment.

She approached the last door and stepped inside, trying her best to mask the footsteps that creaked against the wood floors and threatened to expose her presence. The sensation grew stronger as she approached, pulsing through her body, warming her now in a wave of energy as if she were too close to an electrical transformer.

She was facing a wall or a kind of partition that stood between her and the light. She moved around the corner and spotted Lorelei sitting on the floor with her hands resting on her knees as if in a trance.

Sarah squinted and shielded her eyes as a raging sphere of light hovered in the air only inches from Lorelei's face. The energy held no definite shape; instead, it wavered and transformed like a massive ball of plasma, free from all constraints of time and space. The edges flared like the sun, sparking and rippling.

Lorelei's posture and motionless stance were identical to the way Alex had instructed Sarah to sit in the garden. Lorelei didn't look back or even seem to notice Sarah's presence.

Sarah supposed that Lorelei was a psychic after all, and she was doing her thing. But the sphere of light captivated her. What was it?

As the question lingered in her mind, the shifting flares of light formed the faint outline of a face for just a moment before fading again.

Was this an astral projection of Lorelei's consciousness? Did she have the same gift or training as Alex? Was Lorelei communicating with someone?

In any case, it was clear that Sarah shouldn't have intruded on the woman. She backtracked to the door, taking shallow breaths until after she had shut it behind her, carefully closing the latch.

As she returned to her room, the warm, electrical sensation stopped abruptly. Sarah glanced back. The light streaming from under the door was gone.

※ 18 ※

Jason must have noticed that Emmie was distracted because he grabbed the wheel for the second time and met her gaze as she sped through traffic. "How are you holding up? Do you want me to drive?"

"I'm good." She forced a grin. "Well, no. No, I'm not. I mean, what the hell was that all about? He can't do that to us."

Jason shook his head. "He's obviously going to talk with his friends about all of this behind the scenes."

Emmie growled. "We're the ones who found the image. We're a part of this, whether they want to acknowledge it or not."

Jason nodded. "You're preaching to the choir, Em. Knowing the people he hangs out with, he's probably already busy rounding up his posse and getting their conspirator robes on."

Emmie gripped the steering wheel and made a sharp left turn. "It's their bureaucracy that gets me... and the secrecy."

Jason threw one hand on the dashboard halfway into the turn. "Agreed."

"It'll get buried if we don't do something about it."

"So what do you think we should do?" He glanced at her with a devious grin. "Go back there and rough him up?"

"Ha!" She wouldn't rule it out. They had hit a major road-block, but she was far from giving up. The symbol of the rose stuck in her mind. "Howard said the symbol was a rose. It was obvious he knew more than he was telling us. Have you got any idea what he was talking about?"

"I would need to do some research, but a rose could mean anything. A lot of religious symbols contain roses and flowers. We would need to find some connection to Dr. Albright's organization, but Carey Kali doesn't have anything like that, as far as I know. It's got to be some other group or sect, or maybe even a single person. I just don't know."

Emmie slowed in the heavy traffic. "So we're just going to let it go then? Walk away with our tails between our legs?"

Jason laughed. "Sounds like you already know the answer to that question."

"Damn right." Emmie suddenly veered the car over two lanes of traffic and made a U-turn within the space of a few seconds.

"I think it's my turn to drive," Jason said nervously.

"I got it."

As they headed back to Howard's house, her heart beat faster. The more she thought about what Howard had said to them, the more Jason's idea of roughing up Howard sounded like a viable solution. His words grated through her mind like sandpaper, and she dug her fingernails into the sides of the steering wheel.

The drive back to the man's home took longer than the retreat because of the rush hour traffic, but Emmie was relieved to see that his car was still in the driveway.

"I'm not going to hold back this time." Emmie turned off the engine.

"I'm looking forward to that."

Moments after they stepped out of the car, the windows in Howard's house lit up as if the sun itself had exploded in his living room.

Emmie shielded her eyes, then looked at Jason. His reaction mirrored her own.

"A fire?" she asked.

"Something definitely went wrong."

As they hurried toward the front door, Emmie could only think of the brilliant light that Sarah had become at Whisper House. But this wasn't the same. Certainly not the same intensity or the same beautiful aura. This light was harsh, and it stung her on a deep, psychical level.

Howard must have locked the front door after they'd left, so they circled around to the rear of the house and entered through the unlocked back door. The smell of burning flesh filled the air, the same familiar toxic odor she had smelled while investigating Dr. Albright's condo. A blinding light came from the living room as they covered their eyes and moved closer to the source.

The smoke alarms had gone off, nearly drowning out Howard's guttural cries of pain that seemed to grow louder, although there were no flames.

Emmie caught sight of the light's source a moment before Jason joined her. Howard was lying face up on the floor while a powerful being of light stood over him. The being was sucking a vortex of white-hot flames from Howard's chest and he writhed in pain, convulsing and gasping as it drew his life energy out of him. His cries and struggling escalated then stopped only moments after they spotted him. An incendiary blaze spread over his body and consumed him. The feverish light blackened his flesh, leaving it like charred wood.

The being's light was overwhelming, but Emmie forced herself to stare at it and tried to make sense of its actions and, more importantly, its identity. Its form held no clues, except for the uniquely feminine gestures and the way it extracted Howard's spirit, as if it were enticing a lost puppy to draw closer. The hint of a face appeared within the shifting presence, although it only held a single expression: elation.

Jason rushed forward and pulled at Howard's leg. The man's clothes were remarkably untouched by the light. A moment into his attempt at a rescue, a flash of light struck Jason, knocking him back to the ground.

Their presence jarred the spirit's spiraling connection with Howard, and it moved away while fading.

"You're not going anywhere!" Emmie focused on the form with her eyes closed, pulling at the spirit and holding it in place. If she could just see its identity...

The spirit resisted her efforts to pull it closer, and a wave of energy swept through Emmie just as it had with Jason. But instead of knocking her back, the jolt of energy merged with her spirit. She absorbed the spirit's essence and power.

Even with her eyes closed, she sensed a deep connection with the spirit. The spirit's true form was manifesting in her mind. Her Third Eye, the long-dormant ability to see without seeing, came alive, and she knew that if she focused on the spirit only a little longer, she would have all the answers.

But the light being seemed to focus on her too. It was studying her, calculating her reaction, and they faced each other for a moment before it broke free from Emmie's mental grip and flashed out of the room as if a bolt of lightning had electrified the area and then gone dark.

Emmie scanned the area desperately after it left. It couldn't have gotten away that easily. But it had. They had missed their chance to identify it before it had disappeared.

Jason rushed to Emmie's side as the smoke alarms blared. He pulled at her arm, mouthing the words, "We need to get out of here."

Glancing back at Howard's body, she found that the man had become a charred pile of flesh with only the top of his head and his lower legs surviving the spirit's attack.

That same thing must have happened to Dr. Albright.

Jason pulled her arm again, but she broke free and stepped

closer to Howard's body. She scanned his chest for the one thing that would confirm the link between the two deaths. It was there, sunken and black within the ashes and flesh. The now unmistakable symbol of a rose.

The darkness seemed to go on forever in every direction, with only a wall of mirrors circling Finn as if in a fun house, daring him to find a way out. The floor was a polished black mirror, reflecting his confused, pale face. A row of spot-lights shined down from above as if he stood on a stage with an audience out there watching his every move. Was that a face in the darkness? Someone who'd come to watch the performance?

But... a comedy or a tragedy?

There were only two props on the stage with him, and another actor, his brother, Neil, who cowered on the floor beside a brown leather chair. Finn recognized that chair. The same one Finn had left behind at his parents' house after he'd moved out to go to college. They had found Neil's body beside that chair after the suicide. But now his brother was... alive. The second prop was a pistol wavering in Neil's hand.

Finn reached toward his brother with panic surging through him. "Wait, Neil. Don't do it! Please!"

Neil seemed not to notice, instead raising the pistol to his head as tears streamed down his cheeks.

Finn jumped forward and let out a heart wrenching scream, but it was too late. His brother pulled the trigger.

The blast reverberated throughout Finn's consciousness as if the bullet had struck his own heart. He hadn't reached Neil in time, and he turned away after his brother had completed the act. There was no chance to avoid it. The mirrors surrounding the stage played the tragedy out over and over. Pressing his eyes shut made no difference. Everywhere he turned, he saw the nightmare he had witnessed. A flood of tears poured from his eyes as he sank to the floor. Every spark of life drained out of him, just as his brother's blood drained out over the floor.

As Finn sat on his knees beside his brother, a black void enveloped him. Everything was gone. Everything, except the awareness that he'd failed to save his brother and the intense pain that refused to subside, no matter how much he tried to push it away.

A single spotlight switched on above him, lighting his broken form on the stage. He looked up and stared into the blinding light. It was beautiful, and somehow familiar.

There was something within the light. A face, and wings sprouting off from a center form. An angel.

My angel, Sarah.

He stretched toward her radiant light.

It's exactly how Emmie had described Sarah's light at Whisper House. I couldn't see it then. But he could see her aura now. All her brilliance and colors and warmth. All of it shining down on him. He stood and reached up toward it.

She was coming down with her wings spread and her hands stretched out toward him, and he couldn't wait to embrace her again.

When she arrived, floating above him as an ethereal vision of beauty, she took his hands. "Let me..."

Finn nodded and they rose above the darkness, even as it seemed to drag on him, pulling on something deep in his chest. Something wouldn't let him go. Or *he* wouldn't let something go. But he kept his eyes on Sarah.

"I got you," she assured him in a soft, calm voice.

"You're wasting your time." Finn loosened his grip on her hands.

"No." She tightened her grip.

"It's hopeless." He let go.

He would have fallen back into the darkness except that she held on, her wings fluttering faster and faster to compensate for his struggle to free himself.

"We're almost there, Finn." Sarah gestured toward a bright blue sky above them. "I won't let you go."

"Yes, you will." Finn lurched up at Sarah's left wing, and yanked it down at an odd angle until it snapped. She screamed and he slipped away.

Finn dropped. When he hit the ground, his eyes snapped open and Natalia was staring down at him as he lay on the floor. When he sat up, a crooked smile formed on her face and she spoke in a strained voice, "You did good."

Reality returned. The room was just as it had been before she had drawn him into the vision. The scent of candles filled the room again and the hand-carved wooden tray sat between them on the floor, although the thick black liquid had spilled over the wooden floors and one of the porcelain bowls had shattered.

Had that been the sound of the angel's wing breaking?

No. He now saw that she was nursing her left arm with a pained expression. That had been him. "Did I break it?" he asked anxiously.

"Hardly," she said, rubbing it. "You think you can take down a Cuban girl that easily?"

Finn shook his head, unsure of himself. "What just happened?"

"We took our first step toward building your psychic defenses."

He gestured to her arm. "I'm sorry."

"I know. It's nothing. All part of the process."

Memories of what he'd done at Whisper House flooded back and his heart sank. "But I hurt you."

"Doesn't matter. Who did you see first?"

"Neil."

"Then you saw your girlfriend, right?"

"Yes. She appeared like an angel." He shrugged. "You know, archetypes."

"She seems like all that's good to you, so it figures. The feminine often does that to men because you're very simple and also a bunch of *cabrones.*"

He bowed his head. "Thank you. Doubt I will be seeing you as an angel anytime soon."

"Make it never. Tell me, then you went toward her?"

"Yes. I took her hand, and we started rising out of the darkness. But—"

"You sabotaged yourself."

Finn nodded. "I did. And I... broke her wing."

"Don't you see, though? That's progress. You saw your brother, what causes you pain at first, but you went toward your happiness as I helped to guide your focus."

Again he looked at her arm. "And I tried to attack happiness. How is that progress?"

"Because that's not what you were doing before you came here. You saw your brother first and experienced the tragedy of his death with all the self-defeating survivors' guilt that comes with it. If you don't learn how to rise above that, you will always be psychically vulnerable. But now you see the way out, the love for your girl."

"But it seems that the truth I found in Whisper House isn't going away."

"It never goes away. Not the pain, not the truth, not the love. It all belongs to you, but your pain is what makes you weak. The things that haunt you... control you. That's the key here."

Finn contemplated everything she had said as Natalia cleaned up the mess on the floor. It made sense now, his violent outbursts, but he still had no idea how she planned to fix it.

Natalia took the tray of items and left the room for a short time before returning with a fresh tray with new black porcelain bowls filled with leaves and more black liquid. Returning to her seat in front of Finn, she took his hand again and met his gaze. "Are you ready? Now we'll use what we've learned to strengthen your psychic defenses. Buckle up."

O nce they were safely away from Howard's house, Emmie's racing heart slowed, and so did the speed of her rental car.

She couldn't shake the image of what she had seen earlier. The gruesome image of Howard pinned to the floor and what could only be described as some angel of death hovering over his body, drawing in his spirit.

"At least we know now what we're up against," Jason said.

"How well could you see it?" Emmie asked.

"I don't see ghosts, ever, well... until now, but that thing was right there. Was that a ghost? Do they all look like that to you?"

She shook her head. "I've never encountered something like that before. Not *anything* like the usual spirits I've run across so far. This one had no real appearance, no identity... and no trauma."

"It's no wonder your life is a mess. I would be too, if I had to deal with that every day."

"Well, unless you want to break up, you might be seeing a lot of stuff from now on. Or standing by while I see it." She glanced over. "But thanks for saying that."

"Better late than never, right?" he said softly. "Still, what was that thing doing to Howard?"

The trauma flashed through her mind, but she pushed it away. "Taking his spirit."

"Can they do that?"

"I don't know."

"So what, or who, could it be?" Jason asked. "Is it even dead if I can see it?"

"Don't know either. If only Howard had told us, instead of thinking we were incompetents."

"But maybe if he had told us, that thing might have come for us next."

Thinking about how the spirit had focused on Emmie for a moment sent a chill up her spine now. *It could come for us now because it sure did get a good look at us.* "I guess there's no point in speculating."

Jason turned his attention back to his phone, flipping through several screens before stopping on one. "Let me see if I can find someone else we can talk to about this. Someone *reliable* this time."

"No more talking to anyone. From now on, we'll just do our own research."

Jason shook his head slightly. "We'll need some kind of help, Em. And I know a place—not a person—just a place we can go to sort this out. A library with private rooms to do research. Fortunately for us, we're in New Orleans, the home of vampires, the occult, and ghosts, so there's got to be books that tell us what that thing is. That's why Carey Kali made this area its home."

Emmie scowled at hearing the organization's name. "We'll definitely stay away from them this time."

"Right." Jason glanced at his phone's display again. "Only twenty minutes away. I'm reserving a room now."

"Perfect."

A few moments later, the phone pinged and Jason

announced, "We got it. He has two hours starting in half an hour. Lucky. I'll take the two." After he texted back, he added, "Don't tell Finn or he'll bother me to bring him."

Hearing Finn's name drew Emmie out of her train of thought. His face appeared in her mind, and suddenly she missed him. Despite Jason's knowledge of Carey Kali, artifacts and the history of the occult, Finn was the investigator. Jason was smart, but his expertise was people. Street smarts versus Finn's book smarts. She missed Finn's outside-the-box thinking at that moment, and the endless clatter of his laptop's keyboard from the back seat.

She had the urge to text him. He *was* only a message away, but she wanted to give him the space that he needed to heal.

They arrived at the library twenty minutes later, and this time they didn't need to be let into a private, unmarked place. The name of the shop was in full display outside, The Veiled Spirit. Jason schmoozed with the store owner, a singularly average-looking man who didn't look wealthy as Roger and Howard had done.

As their chat continued for several minutes, Emmie attempted to grasp the enormity of the place. The books were stacked to the ceiling—literally to the ceiling, as though the place would collapse if you removed even a single one—with shelves covering every wall and crevice. Someone had even modified an arched doorway leading to a side room with a stack of old hardcovers fitted together to look like the stones of a Roman archway. Small white signs were posted along every shelf around the room, identifying the subjects that covered everything occult, from Tarot cards to astrology, passing through creatures of legend and psychic phenomena.

But her spirits sank as she looked at the clientele: girls giggling in a corner while they perused a Zodiac love-compatibility book, middle-aged women wearing large jewelry and picking through sorcery texts, a pale young man sitting and reading about vampires, and a couple holding hands and looking at books on Tantric sex.

Not sure Finn would be impressed...

But Jason seemed to guess what she was thinking, as he had been watching her with a secret smile. After assisting the middle-aged ladies with their choice of sorcery information, the owner beckoned and led them to the back of the store. Tons of books were packed into just that small space, which extended no more than ten feet in any direction.

Yet, instead of stopping in that room, the store owner continued past those books and moved aside a stray ladder to reveal a door at the far side. He opened it with a key and stepped aside. "They're in here."

He flipped on the light in the closet-sized space. There was only enough room for one of them to go in at a time. The walls were hidden behind rows and rows of old leather-bound books, the kind Emmie had only seen in places like Betty's or in a museum. Other volumes were newer.

He beckoned again and opened another door beyond the books into a room that held a table and lamp. "This is where you can do your reading. It's cold, but I have no heating here. Fluctuations in temperature are bad for these old books. And you can't take them to the front; they're not for everyone."

"All right. Should I pay you for the two hours now?"

"When you leave. And you have to be finished by then because others are coming. My customers are punctual, and I have to be as well."

"Sure, then we won't waste any time," Jason said. "Where are the books I asked about?"

The store owner made a narrow circling gesture with his finger over Jason's right shoulder. "Should be in that area." He expanded the gesture. "But you might want to keep searching over this as well. You know how it is, one thing leads to the other..."

Once the owner left and closed the door, Emmie locked it

and they removed their coats, dropping them in the private reading room. Emmie shivered in the cold air but wearing a coat while searching through the volumes would slow them down. Jason pulled one of the books from the area the owner had indicated and began flipping through it with great care.

"Two hours?" Emmie glanced at all the books. "That's not enough time."

"We'll need to be fast." Jason plucked another book off the shelf and handed it to her. "Just start reading, looking at the index if the book has one. The good thing here is that it's all divided by subject, so if we find anything like that creature of death there, then it might mention more things, and we have other books to look through."

Emmie flipped through the pages. "We need to find anything that looks like the rose we saw. Or anything that mentions a vampire ghost, stealing energy or burning. Anything like that."

After only a few minutes, Jason carried one book back to the table in the secret reading room and sat down with it, using his phone to flip through websites if he found some term or concept he needed to clarify. Emmie leaned against the doorway with her own book. Lots on ghosts in that one. Japanese ghosts, African ghost tales, demons of all sorts.

Jason said after a little while, "There is some stuff covering what I think we saw, like an incubus, sitting on someone's chest, stealing his soul."

Emmie shook her head. "The one we saw was female. So it was more like a succubus."

"You know your demons."

"I guess I picked up a little knowledge from hanging around Finn."

"So, could it have been a demon?" Jason asked. "It didn't seem to have a body."

Both made a face of discovery, and Emmie turned to the shelves again. "That's right, ethereal."

She started reading through titles as Jason got up and approached.

"I said angel of death, but it was more like a devil. A vampire... definitely not an angel."

"I don't think you should discount your first impression," Jason said. "They gave strange names to things back then. Angels could be seen as vengeful creatures, like in the Old Testament. Plus, you're psychic, so we can't discard your intuition."

Emmie grimaced. "I don't think it works like that."

"But some gifts probably bleed into others. And who knows if this type of visitation started as something positive, like what Sarah does when people die, guiding their souls to the light, and then became something bad?"

Emmie thought about Howard, warning them away, and then pictured the spirit's blinding energy and the way it had attacked her without success after striking down Jason. She considered how hard it would be to make a ghost like that pass on. *That thing would resist like hell.*

"If it is a conjured spirit," Jason said, taking more books, "we need to un-conjure it."

"Just like *that?*" She snapped her fingers. "You make it sound so simple."

"I'm sure it's not simple, but I saw you stand up to it. Maybe if you had gotten the chance to face it down..."

"I didn't so much as stand up to it as I couldn't run away. Luckily, it couldn't strike me down, for whatever reason, but it was clear that it wanted to."

"You're more powerful than that thing," Jason said, putting his free arm around her waist.

"I highly doubt that."

"It was kind of sexy to see you so brave."

"Maybe it just didn't know how to deal with me." She smiled at him. "And don't encourage me."

"I just know what you're capable of when you get mad. You tried to staple my face once. Remember that?"

She let out a big laugh, suddenly remembering the moment from her childhood. "You haven't seen anything yet." Emmie pushed him away. "Read! We have an hour and a half now."

There was an overwhelming amount of information to process, and some of it was so complex and hard to read on many levels. The old English words took time to *translate,* and then she strained to understand some of the descriptions and the many odd references to other books. How could anyone be expected to sift through so much information in such a short amount of time?

She looked over at Jason, who had taken a few books with him to the table and still switched between books and the internet.

Finn would do it faster than them. He would just know what piece of information really mattered.

But Finn's not here.

They sifted through a pile of books, ignoring pangs of thirst and hunger because their time was limited. Every now and again they would mention something to each other and start a new search, but they were still far from discovering what the rose meant.

Finally, they had whittled down their time to a little over half an hour.

Emmie stared at Jason, who was still sitting at the table glancing between his phone and an open book in front of him. "We need help."

He glanced over at her. "Who do you have in mind?"

"Well, there's no way I'm asking anyone from Carey Kali to help with this. Howard proved that we can't trust anyone anymore."

He raised his palms and went back to the book. The store owner opened the door to the rare-book closet and reminded them they had only a short time left before the next customers arrived.

Jason called out, "Can we come back after the next customer leaves? I'll make it worth your while."

"Can't," the store owner said firmly. "Have a family thing tonight and won't miss it. And I'm sorry, but I'm pretty booked for the rest of the week. You're lucky there was a cancellation."

He left, and Emmie looked at all the books they still needed to get through. And already her eyes and head hurt. She didn't have Finn's persistent intellect for this sort of thing, and she couldn't stop thinking of him.

After Jason let out an exasperated sigh and closed the book he'd been reading, Emmie made a decision. Stepping out of the room on the other side with the excuse that she needed a little air, she stood in the bigger public area and checked her text messages. There were some from both Finn and Sarah. Sarah wrote about feeling empowered, talking of herself as a *door of light*. This sounded slightly worrying, but Emmie couldn't say why. She read Finn's message, in which he reassured her that he was finally starting to face his demons.

Emmie responded to him by attaching the picture of the rose she'd taken at Dr. Albright's home and wrote, *How would you go about discovering what an image like this means? It's supposed to be a rose.*

21

A t first, Sarah didn't recognize the ball of brown fur cupped in Alex's hands when he presented it to her. Only after glimpsing its face did she see that it was a chunky rabbit. Either sleeping or...

"What's that?" Sarah asked.

"Your next project."

They had trained for several hours that morning, and Alex had praised her successes, calling her "a natural," which only stirred her desire to push herself even further. He had chosen an area of the garden a little closer to the house, but it didn't help that Lorelei was watching them with a frown from the back porch. The woman's bandages now covered both her arms. One of the gauze pads hung loose along one corner, and Sarah saw that it wasn't a cut, as Lorelei had said. It looked red and raw. Maybe she'd scalded herself with hot water?

Now Sarah stared at the rabbit, wondering, hoping the thing might move and prove her suspicion wrong. But she knew the truth. The blood had coagulated along the fur where something had injured it, and as Alex sat down and displayed the rabbit between them, she spotted the open wound. The rabbit wasn't moving or breathing. No aura appeared in or around the animal.

What's the point? "It's... dead."

"Correct." He rotated the rabbit in his hands then again placed it on the ground between them, almost with reverence. "This was one of Cecilia's pets. The groundskeeper found it dead in its pen this morning. Something must've slipped in."

Sarah was sorry for Cecilia. "Does she know?"

"Yes, she's quite upset. Devastated."

He seemed to curiously examine the rabbit's wound, without much sympathy.

"You've gone so far so fast," he said. "And with such an amazing natural gift, you can still repair this animal's wound."

Her eyes flew from the animal to Alex's face. Was he serious? "But... it's dead," she repeated.

His expression didn't change. "It's no different from any other wounded animal."

Her eyes widened. "This is a *lot* different."

"It only died hours ago."

Sarah focused on the rabbit for a moment, scanning it for any signs of an aura. If there was even the slightest hint of life in it, she might have a chance, but there was nothing. "Its spirit is gone. I can't possibly do anything with it."

He stared into her eyes. "You are the door of light. The door goes both ways. Do you understand?"

The intensity behind his gaze sent a chill through her. He had never looked at her like that before. She leaned back. "That's not how this works."

"You don't know that, Sarah. If you were to look at the literature again, you'd see that it's exactly how it works." Alex stroked the rabbit's fur as if he were trying to soothe its fears. "This is the next step. The most important one, and it will require all your energy, all your focus. Remember when you were at Whisper House? That's what I want you to become now. The door of light. Find the rabbit's spirit and draw it back from wherever it is."

"I didn't do that, Alex. I sent spirits on. I didn't bring them back. It's not possible."

"It *is* possible. Just remember how it was. It's all I'm asking you."

Sarah tried to remember everything that she had done at Whisper House before becoming the door of light. What had she done there to make so many spirits pass through her light into the next life? The rabbit had died tragically, judging from the wound—but no, this wasn't the same as anything she had done before.

"Sarah, it is the next natural step..."

"It doesn't feel natural."

"You'll know," he said softly. "Don't you always know? Try it."

She didn't believe it, but he had guided her through so much already, and she had grown by leaps and bounds. She closed her eyes, ready to stop if anything didn't feel right, and directed the light within her to grow. After a minute, she let out an exasperated sigh and shook her head. "I don't see it."

Again, Alex stared at her for a moment. "We'll try something else."

Relief swept through her. At least Alex was starting to understand her limitations. She wasn't a miracle worker.

He stood and went into the house, leaving the dead rabbit on the ground in front of her. Its fur bristled in the light breeze. Death was a part of life, and it spared not even a delicate creature such as this.

Only a minute later, Alex returned to the porch with Cecilia at his side. Sarah gasped. What was he doing? She'd be very upset at seeing her rabbit! He sat her in one of the outdoor chairs where she had a clear view of Sarah, propping her up with a large cushion. Lorelei now watched them all with a grim expression, apparently liking her sister's presence even less than Sarah did.

"You should leave her out of it," Lorelei cried to her brother.

He ignored her and hurried back to Sarah, moving with a

determination he'd somehow lacked before. Now Cecilia rocked back and forth in the chair and watched Sarah.

How can that *help?*

Alex returned to his previous place in front of Sarah and gestured to the rabbit. "Let's try it a little differently this time."

"Alex, I'm not sure what you expect of me."

Alex still held that confidence in his stare. "Focus on my sister." He grinned. "The nice one."

Sarah turned and met Cecilia's gaze. So much pain behind those eyes. The effects of the woman's debilitating stroke magnified the distress of losing her pet rabbit. "Her pain, you mean?" she asked, outraged.

"Not the loss, but the love. Her love is like a light, and you are also light. Absorb it, expand it, flow with it like you did with the plants and the bird you healed."

Cecilia's cry of distress, wordless and haunting, made Sarah close her eyes and follow the instructions. She found the love in Cecilia, just as Alex had described, plenty of it pouring out toward her deceased pet. Sarah sensed the stream of pure light that stretched out from the porch and passed into the dead rabbit. "I see it now."

"Grab it."

Sarah did. She expanded her consciousness further and crossed through Cecilia's light. A powerful, painful flash filled her mind, pushing her to the brink of passing out. She must have lost her balance for a moment because Alex held her arm as she steadied herself.

She kept her eyes shut without breaking her focus on the light.

"Did you connect with it?" Alex asked.

Sarah nodded, holding the precious emotion within her spirit like a delicate flower. Assimilating Cecilia's light took far more effort than she had expected. Her mind ached as she attuned to Cecilia's. Something like a migraine flared at the back of her neck, and a strange vibration pulsed through her body as if she might shatter. Her own light seemed to resist the intrusion as they merged, but after the initial interference, the combined light did grow brighter.

Merged within Cecilia's love, the energies swept along, cascading through her and into the rabbit's carcass. She magnified the light at the same time. Just a little of her light was all it took to alter it. The greater her focus, the greater the love pouring out toward the animal.

A warmth swelled around her.

"I can see the door." There was excitement in Alex's voice. "You are becoming the being of light now."

Within the waves of light, the connection to the rabbit's spirit was there, and she reached toward it, extending her light as a single beam of sunshine. The connection jarred her energy as the rabbit's spirit followed her trail of light back to its body. There was still a thin thread of energy connecting its body to its spirit. The cord hadn't been cut entirely yet.

She moved the rabbit's spirit down into its lifeless body through the slender connection and held her breath until something snapped within it. The fusion of its spirit and the physical form crackled to life. Its aura merged with her own light as the body came alive. Still, she held her eyes shut.

Cecilia gasped on the porch and took a deep, broken breath. Sarah heard it even from that distance and felt the shudder in the energy.

Was Cecilia crying?

The moment the rabbit's spirit entered its body and came to life, the result was real and overwhelming. The animal screeched and fluttered in the grass.

"You did it! Oh my God, you did it!" Alex's voice was full of elation.

Sarah opened her eyes. Within the light that still surrounded her, Alex was crying. His voice cracked as tears streamed down his cheeks. "I can't believe this." He wiped away the tears. "I'm so sorry. I can't help myself. This is amazing. It's finally happening."

Sarah turned to face Cecilia. Tears were streaming down the young woman's face as well. But were they tears of joy?

The rabbit convulsed for a short time on its side then flopped upright and wobbled for a moment. The wound had healed completely, although the bloodstains were still there. Its frightened gaze darted from Alex to Sarah. She could feel its confusion. Within seconds, it hopped a few times and paused before sprinting away toward the deep grass at the edge of the garden.

Instead of showing joy or even looking toward her pet, Cecilia hunched forward and rocked back and forth.

"What did I just do?" Sarah felt a sense of wrong hitting her like a blow as she watched the rabbit escape until it disappeared in the tall grass.

Alex seemed not to have heard her question, his face glowing with a deep joy that became stronger even as her own light faded. "It's a miracle," he said. He got to his feet in a flash and almost ran toward the house without looking back. He passed Cecilia without saying a word, rushing inside, and Lorelei followed him.

Cecilia still watched Sarah from the porch, but now she was shaking her head. Even from that distance, Sarah heard Cecilia's voice.

"No, no, no. There is an order to things."

22

F inn's phone pinged, but he hesitated to answer it. Although the psychic blocking training was exhausting, he still hadn't completed everything that Natalia had demanded of him. Reading his messages might derail his focus.

But she had allowed him a thirty-minute break for a meal, so he skimmed through the phone's messages, just to see what his friends were up to. Still nothing from Sarah, but he hadn't written either. He suppressed a sigh and, moving to Emmie, he saw she had sent him a strange photo. He read her message and studied the image curiously, then wrote back. *Weird-looking for a rose. Off the top of my head, roses and other flowers are usually emblems, like something from a noble house. And some religions. And some religious sects. It strikes me that they styled the rose to look like a house sigil.*

Only seconds later, Natalia informed him that his break was over. He left his phone on the kitchen counter and went to meet her at what he now called "the torture chamber."

They trained for the rest of the evening, well into dark, and he came away from the psychic-blocking process exhausted. The hours of intense mental work had forced him to face his deepest fears to identify his triggers.

"That's where the real battle takes place," she had said. "Within your subconscious; that's where they creep in."

So she had relentlessly driven him through the process, each time gradually building a perimeter around his spirit like an alarm system that would trip in his mind at the first sign of an intrusion.

"You will have something like a sixth sense," she had clarified. "But don't think this is a psychic ability. No, it's a suit of armor, like a soldier preparing for hand-to-hand combat. And when you sense the attack begin, remember what you've learned in these moments. When your fears are triggered, the self-destructive tendencies may also return, but you have a guiding light now."

"Sarah's light."

"Correct."

And through the visions she induced, using the black liquid and the leaves, he had come to an understanding with himself, a practical method of clinging to the guiding light in his mind that represented Sarah's love. He had stopped sabotaging himself in the visions, beginning to embrace the fears and trauma with self-forgiveness and acceptance.

"Congratulations." Natalia hugged him after he awoke from his trance. "You intercepted some psychic intrusion."

"Does this mean I'm cured?"

"I said some. Not nearly all."

He groaned. "Do I at least get a gold star, please?"

"Bronze."

Finn shifted in his seat. "That's not good enough to return home."

"No." Natalia gave him a sassy smile. "You're like a psychic boy toy for me now. I'll keep poking at you. But I think you just like to be here, anyway."

He did, but something else must have gone across his face—like how much he missed the girls—because Natalia's eyes sharpened, then softened, and she asked, "What is she like?"

"Who?" Finn countered innocently.

"Your *girlfriend,*" Natalia said in his face, and let out a big laugh.

Finn pushed his eyelids together for a moment. It was useless to repeat that Sarah wasn't his girlfriend. And Natalia, the generous Circe of Cuba, made him want to talk.

"She's beautiful, in every way. I can't describe her, but she's like the sun... She makes me wish I was psychic."

"Why is that?"

"So I could see her the way that Emmie sees her, as the being of light that she became at Whisper House."

Natalia focused on him a little more. "What do you mean?"

"Before we left there, she became this passage, from what Emmie described. Even I could see, I guess on a subconscious level, that she was more radiant than usual, but I wish I could see Sarah like Emmie can, as pure light."

"No one is that."

"Emmie said it was the greatest light she'd ever seen, as Sarah drew all the trapped souls in the house to her, passing through her in joy..."

Natalia's face looked pale, and her mouth gaped. "The door of light. I can't believe it."

"I'm telling you—"

"No, no. Wait."

Natalia stood and left the room, returning with two books, opening them one at a time and showing Finn photos of tintype etchings and pointing at several paragraphs that described what she had just called the door of light. The text went into detail about the origin of the concept, dating it back to the early fourteenth century, referencing another block of medieval English.

A witness of that time described it as:

Behold, 'twas a wondrous vision to see! A woman of light did appear, clad in robes of shimmering gold, radiating a brilliant and celestial glow. Her appearance was fair, with a face full of majesty and grace. Her eyes sparkled like those of the brightest in heaven, and her hair was as threads of the purest silver. Truly, she did seem as though a messenger of the divine had come down to earth to deliver tidings of great importance to mortal men.

Finn read through everything she pointed out, with so much of it seeming like a reference to how Emmie had described Sarah. Its "radiant form," its "golden light serving as a beacon," its "holy aura." All of it came together in his mind like pieces of a puzzle.

Natalia continued, "Those people I studied in the weird house I told you about were so obsessed with finding this. They thought the door of light might be their youngest daughter, so they ran a bunch of experiments to find out, without success. Finn..." She turned his face toward her with both hands. "Finn, if your girl is this door of light, then she is what everyone in the psychic world would love to get their hands on."

"Why?"

"Because she is pure, measureless, once-in-a-generation power! A medium that becomes a doorway between this world and the next."

Finn's mind flashed back to everything Owl Cromwell had talked about at Whisper House—all the texts he'd read discussing portals and lights and dimensions.

And Sarah... She hadn't texted in a long time. Even Emmie hadn't said anything about Sarah in a while. Too long. Where *had* she gone, as a matter of fact? *To find herself...* Florida, but—

"What's the name of the house?" Finn asked.

"Temper House."

"And where is it?"

"St. Augustine. Florida."

"Florida?" Finn swallowed and scrambled to stand. "I'm sorry. I need to—"

He rushed out of the room to get his phone. Maybe it was nothing. He *prayed* it was nothing, but he needed to contact someone to find out what he needed to know, and that might not be Emmie, who had probably sworn some sort of secrecy to

Sarah. He called Sarah's mom. She answered on the second ring, and after a brief exchange she admitted that Sarah was away and had asked her not to tell anyone where she was at.

"I respect that," Finn said. "But this is important."

"Is she in danger?"

"I don't know," he said. "Listen, you don't have to betray her confidence, but if I get it right, just say yes, okay?"

Her mother agreed.

"Did she go to St. Augustine in Florida?"

Sarah's mother gasped. "How did you know?"

❧ 23 ❧

E mmie checked her phone. They didn't have much time left to scour through all the books in the shop owner's private library. It didn't help that he now stood in the doorway of the small room and tapped his fingers against the doorframe, watching them with a steady, curious gaze.

"You've got fifteen minutes," he reminded them.

The man's impatience grated on Emmie's nerves. She glanced up at him and nodded. "Thank you."

He left, but she hadn't found what she was looking for and needed more time. Jason sat beside her, flipping through several websites on his phone and reading without saying a word.

Just as she was about to despair, Emmie's phone pinged with a new message from Finn. She read it.

"Maybe the rose is associated with a house?" she told Jason.

He tilted his head and stared back with a blank expression. "What kind of house?"

Emmie turned her eyes to the private library in the closet. "I saw a book on houses here."

"You mean haunted?"

Without answering him, she stood and walked inside the

book closet again, brushing her finger across each book that she had scanned earlier. "I remember…"

Her finger stopped on one titled, very simply, *A History of Psychic Houses*. She had ignored it before, not knowing how it could be relevant to their search and thinking, like Jason, that it might be a history of haunted houses. No, it was what she might need: a history of *houses passing psychic powers through generations*.

She pulled it out and flipped through the pages as Jason came to stand beside her. A treasure trove of information was in her hands, perhaps outlining most people they needed to distrust… or trust. But they had no time to sort through it all. So many photos of black and white Victorian houses and people, each meticulously described in blocky paragraphs of detail.

"Do you remember any of this? We studied some of these people with Dr. Albright, but I never paid much attention at the time."

"I know something, but… the rose?"

She skimmed ahead and scanned by chapter titles, narrowing down her search quickly. "A lot of these houses are in Europe. Mostly old families passing psychic genes and that sort of thing. Lineage stuff going back generations."

Jason looked back. The owner had left the door open, now that it was past closing time, and he was only waiting for private clients. He was reminding them they had ten minutes left.

The man gave them no privacy now, but she forced herself to ignore the pressure. She remembered what Jason had said about an index and found it at the end. The names of the houses were organized alphabetically, with each house displaying their sigils below the name. Searching through references, she found one to a rose. There it was.

Temper House.

She tapped the symbol: It was what they had seen at Albright's, and even more clearly in what had remained of Howard. "That's it."

Jason looked over her shoulder. "Wow…"

"Finn, you're a genius," Emmie mumbled.

"I would have found that eventually," Jason said with hurt in his voice.

Emmie patted his hand. "I know."

Huddling together, they read the description of the house. The Tempers had traveled from Scotland to the United States in 1920 and settled in Florida. Emmie skimmed through the information that covered several key topics, mentioning a prized sprawling zoo on their property and the exceptional psychic skills of a family capable of astral projections. The Tempers had set up a small school for psychics, which had flourished for decades.

It was closed in 2008, after the death of Stuart and Patricia Temper. They had left three children who did not continue their work.

"Stuart Temper..." Jason nodded and ran into the small reading room. He returned to her with a book and showed her an open page. It was the transcription of a lecture given in 1997, entitled *Properties of the Door of Light*.

The door of light.

Astral projections.

Emmie's heart raced as she took out her phone and scrolled through Sarah's message.

"I'm afraid—" said the owner, coming to the door again.

"Not now!" Emmie roared and slammed the door in his face.

Jason looked shellshocked. "I think I just lost a few of my contacts on this trip..."

"You don't understand," she told Jason. "Sarah has been talking of doors of light and astral projection. And she is in *Florida*... Where there is a school dealing with all that."

Jason's alarmed expression spoke louder than words. "Astral projections. Like—that thing we saw? You said it was alive."

An astral projection, not a ghost... Could that be it? She clutched Jason's arm, a wave of heat sweeping over her then turning cold. *Sarah!* "It's got to be a coincidence, right?"

He spoke in a soft, serious tone, "I don't believe in them."

Emmie dialed Sarah's number with trembling hands. No answer. Then she dialed Finn, but his number went straight to his voicemail. Her panic rose, but she left him a simple, urgent message: "Call me. It's about Sarah."

The frustration welled up inside her as she tugged on Jason's arm. "We have to drive to St. Augustine. Tonight."

❧ 24 ❧

Sarah struggled to her feet and stood in place as she gathered her strength. Alex had left Cecilia alone with Sarah. The odd sister kept looking toward the grass where the rabbit had disappeared.

"Fluffy," Cecilia called out in a sweet childlike voice. "Little Bo Peep lost her sheep—" Cecilia mumbled in her sweet voice.

"—and doesn't know where to find them," Sarah finished. "Is that why you keep saying that? You've lost your pet? I'll try to find it."

Cecilia continued mumbling beneath her breath. She had seemed distressed when the rabbit came to life, but now wanted it? Sarah was exhausted, but she was curious too. She scanned the grass. Lots of places to hide, but the rabbit couldn't have gotten very far. The tight fence around the property would prevent it from escaping, and she still held a connection with the rabbit, although it had almost completely faded. The animal's emotions reverberated enough for her to locate it without too much difficulty.

Sarah followed the trail of emotions as Cecilia continued repeating the pet's name from the porch.

"Fluffy..." Cecilia said in a sweet voice. "Little Bo Peep..."

Sarah's body ached as if she had just run a marathon, but she trudged ahead and scoured the taller grass and hedges for any sign of the revived Fluffy.

It's not too far away. Its presence stood out in her mind clearly —its light had almost burned a permanent impression against the back of her eyes only minutes earlier—but it was hiding now, and scared.

"Come here, little guy," she said softly, as if somehow that might lure it out of hiding. "Your mommy misses you."

A cool breeze swept in and bristled the grass and trees around her. Something shifted ahead.

"Fluffy? Get back here, little critter. We don't want you to get hurt again."

A patch of weeds shifted and a twig cracked several yards ahead. Sarah stepped around one of the flowering garden plants and through a sprawling section of tall grass. Something was moving straight ahead, at the edge of a small clearing by one of the animal enclosures.

The brown outline of a rabbit came into view.

Fluffy.

It had moved out from behind a patch of grass and sat frozen in place with its little chest heaving in and out. She inched forward, lowering herself and moving closer as the rabbit stiffened.

It's terrified.

And it's getting ready to run.

She held out her hand as if offering it a bit of food, like she would to a shy cat. She whispered, "Here, little guy."

The bond between them grew stronger as she tried to move even closer, although there was no way to help it understand her thoughts.

Its primal instincts took over. Fluffy darted off into a thicker section of grass beside the fence and she lost sight of it.

"Damn." She glanced back toward the house and Cecilia was

still on the porch, watching with wide eyes. "I'm not Dr. Doolittle here," Sarah said under her breath.

Sarah tried again, calling out the rabbit's name a few times as she followed it into a shady section at the edge of the property. Each time she spotted it, the thing would dart off in a new direction. It seemed to move faster than Sarah, but then she was so tired... She had put so much effort into reviving it.

A strange disturbance erupted from the grass where the rabbit had disappeared. A squeal, then a flurry of activity filled the air as if two cats were fighting. She stayed back, and after only a few seconds the noises stopped, although she already knew what had happened.

Her connection with the rabbit had abruptly ended.

Something got it.

Maybe just as well. None of this felt right. Even Cecilia knew that, she was sure.

She moved forward with more caution now, using her foot to push aside the grass and tall weeds at the place where she had last seen the rabbit.

A large bush beyond the weeds shuddered as an animal lurched out toward her. The thing charged at her shoe first, biting into it and throwing an outstretched paw along the side and bottom, catching its claw in the rubber sole for a moment before releasing it.

Sarah jumped back even as the thing retreated into the tall grass again.

It looked like a large cat. But its color was all wrong. Its eyes were sunken and glassy, and the right side of its face drooped as if it had started to rot. The left side of its face was stretched thin and wrapped against its skull as if its muscles had melted away. Its matted fur was muddy and streaked with blood, obscuring its true colors, although the dark spots were there. A frayed rope was tied around its neck, with one end dangling. It was a bobcat.

As Sarah moved back, the bobcat paraded out from hiding with the bloody rabbit hanging from its jaws. It stepped sideways, although it wobbled with each step as one of its back paws dragged behind it, limp and broken. It moved in brief spurts, stumbling and shaking the dead rabbit in its mouth while its gaze locked onto her.

The bobcat dropped the rabbit and limped toward her, keeping pace as she stepped back.

She could feel its cold thirst. *It wants me next.*

No time to analyze anything. Sarah turned and ran. Her heart pounded, but she forced her exhausted body to run faster. The bobcat's footsteps thudded in the grass only a few yards behind her as the back of the house came into view. She gasped with each breath and tried to scream, but only a guttural cry came out.

Cecilia was still there, still watching with wide eyes—but what could she do?

It will get me.

Lorelei charged out of the back door with a rifle. She pointed it directly at Sarah, then shifted it slightly to the left before firing it.

The first blast hit the grass behind Sarah's foot, and she didn't slow down. The second blast exploded against the bobcat. The animal let out a wild screech, although its footsteps continued toward Sarah.

Now Sarah glanced back. The bright sunlight brought out all the imperfections and twisted reality of the animal that had been chasing her.

Bobcat or not, it was dead, and it had been dead a long time. But it was still moving, and it struggled to keep pace with her. The thing dragged its body along with its front paws until Lorelei walked over to it, seemingly unbothered by the attack, pressed the rifle against the animal's head and fired.

❧ 25 ❧

F inn stepped outside into the sunshine, but it wasn't the ocean's gentle breeze that filled his mind. Sarah was in trouble. Despite the distance between him and his friends, he felt a deep need to be with them at that moment. It didn't matter if he hadn't finished developing his psychic defenses or not. Who knew how long that would take?

He took out his phone, switched it back on and checked his messages. There were several notifications, and the first name he spotted jumped out at him.

Emmie.

Reading the several messages she'd sent him made him break out into a cold sweat.

He dialed her number and started talking as soon as she answered. "Emmie, listen to me, what you found out about Temper House. Natalia knows it. She was there once. Sarah is in that town. Do you know whether she went to that house?"

"Sarah isn't answering her phone. But, Finn, why else would she have gone to that same place?" Emmie's voice wavered. "I'm on my way there now, but how soon can you get to St. Augustine?"

"I'm on an island. It will depend on flights, and getting

through the airports is the biggest bottleneck."

"You might still get there before us," Emmie said. "We're several hours away by car. Let's just get there, Finn."

"Em." He forced himself to restrain the emotions welling up in his throat. "If something happened—"

"I know, Finn," Emmie said, "And me too. Same. We'll get through this together."

Together.

For the first time since Whisper House, he considered himself part of the team again. "We will."

He ended the call. It wouldn't take him long to get back to the airport and land in Florida if there was a flight leaving soon, but there was still suffocating apprehension in his chest. The barriers he had set within himself to not return until he was absolutely cured of whatever had caused him to act dangerously at Whisper House crumbled when he'd discovered that he hadn't been there to help Sarah. He'd gone too far in the other direction.

Natalia had joined him so silently that when she touched his shoulder, he jumped.

"Do you need to leave?"

He stared out at the wispy clouds along the horizon. "Yes. My friend is in that house. Temper House."

"Calm down, Finn. The Tempers would never harm the door of light. She's too precious."

"She's too precious to *me*, and I can't take the chance that someone might take advantage of her."

Natalia looked concerned but sympathetic. "I understand— but if they want Sarah and you go back, you might face the same type of dark entities that you encountered at Whisper House. They might see you as a threat to them."

"I've learned something," he said, almost begging for her to reassure him.

"Not enough, Finn."

He craved her guidance and generosity—almost depended on

them now—but he knew in his bones where he should be.

"I would never forgive myself if anything happened to her while I was here."

Natalia nodded, then took his face in her hands, the way she did when she wanted him to really understand something. "Just fill your mind with everything I showed you."

A silence passed between them, and he saw that she had something in her hand. She extended it toward him in her open palm. It was a small, flat piece of black stone attached to a silver necklace. He recognized it by its texture and color right away. An obsidian stone.

"Don't really love obsidian stones."

"It's not what you think. The larger flat pieces are used as a window to the spirit world—yes—but this charm has no intrinsic magical properties, good or bad. It's something for you to focus on, to remember our training."

Finn scooped it out of her hand. He felt its odd weight and jagged edges between his fingers. "Thank you."

"If I can't be there to help, at least think of this stone as something from me to guide you." She sighed. "And if there's only one thing you remember from your time here, make it this: that dark magic cannot enter a mind full of light and joy. Shadows can't hide when the sun shines in every direction. Let that be your biggest lesson for this visit."

He looked at her with gratitude, and it was his turn to cradle her face. "You are a being of light too, Natalia," he said. "We may not be finished here, but you have given me so much more than you can know. If I had met you a few months ago—"

"Who says I'd want you, *engreído?*" she said and let out her lovely laugh. "You really think you're God's gift to women, Finn Adams."

They embraced as she added, "Come back, you silly. I'll always help you."

Her last advice echoed in his mind as he headed toward the airport.

26

The bobcat was dead.

But had it been alive?

Its dull eyes had stared back at her, but had it *seen* her?

Dead things don't move like that. They don't move at all. It didn't take a medical degree to understand that.

But what kind of degree would it take to explain what had happened with the rabbit? She had brought it back from dead; she was sure of it.

There is an order to things... Cecilia had said that, and she hadn't been happy about the rabbit returning.

Sarah trudged back to the house, keeping her gaze on the back door. She expected Alex to appear after the gunshots. Where had he gone? The *miracle* that Alex had expected so strongly had ended in tragedy, and the thought of the rabbit's second fate, this time in the clutches of that emaciated bobcat, nauseated her as she stepped onto the porch.

Lorelei followed her, swinging the rifle at her side. "Can't have wild animals like that threatening our guests."

Sarah glanced at her. The woman had a huge smile on her face—pure joy, for once, instead of her usual sarcasm. "What...

was that? It had a rope around its neck. Did it escape from your zoo?"

"You think it looked like one of ours? We don't keep disgusting things like that."

Some of the bandages around Lorelei's forearm had been removed, exposing a large patch of red skin. Definitely burn marks.

Lorelei joined Cecilia, who was still watching them silently from the porch. "Honey peas, you need to go to your meditation room. I know you're upset, so I'll join you there in a bit with some great aromas and we'll put on some music. You want to meditate with me?" Lorelei caressed her sister's back, then helped her to stand and ushered her inside while holding the door open. Turning back, Lorelei made a wide gesture for Sarah to enter. "After you..."

Sarah stepped inside, watching Cecilia move obediently to the meditation room in the back.

Lorelei nudged Sarah forward without aggression and walked beside her, carrying the rifle in both hands as if preparing to fire it at a moment's notice. "I think the best way to celebrate your little escape from the big, bad kitty cat is to join me in the kitchen for a drink."

The thought of drinking or eating anything at that moment nauseated Sarah, but she didn't want to say it. Best not to show any weakness to that woman. "I'm not very thirsty."

"Because you're in shock. And you're a nurse—you know a little drink might avoid hysterics later. We have some good scotch, just the thing."

"Where did Alex go?" Sarah asked while glancing around.

Lorelei rolled her eyes. "He's too emotional sometimes."

"What is he emotional about?"

Ignoring the question, Lorelei led Sarah back to the kitchen and pulled out a chair at the table along the way, nodding at it. "Have a seat."

The woman grabbed a decanter from the pantry and three

heavy glasses, pouring one for each of them and setting the third glass beside Sarah before sitting down across from her.

Lorelei raised her glass and drank. "Here's to surviving."

Sarah took a few sips of the scotch before Alex came down the stairs, entered the kitchen and stood beside them.

Though his eyes were wide, watery and red, his face was full of elation. "You did so wonderful out there."

"Did you see what happened afterwards?" she asked.

"I heard the rifle go off." He sat beside Sarah and opposite Lorelei, pulling the glass to him. "So, what was it this time?" Alex asked Lorelei.

"One of the bobcats."

"I thought—" Sarah cleared her throat. "I thought the fence wouldn't allow any wild animals in."

The siblings exchanged a glance, and for the first time there was complicity in it. They shared a secret; maybe many. And Alex didn't try to reassure her as he usually did.

"Must have slipped through..." he mumbled, twirling his glass.

Sarah pushed aside the scotch. It had a strange salty taste.

"You should have more," Lorelei said. She told Alex, "After all, she almost got taken down by one of your abominations."

Sarah furrowed her brows and met Alex's gaze. "One of yours?"

"My bully of a sister likes to blame everything on me," he said.

"*Was* it yours?"

Alex touched Sarah's shoulder and glanced down at her clothes. "It didn't hurt you..."

"No."

"I'm very sorry that happened. I shouldn't have left you out there alone, but I didn't want you to see me—"

"—blubbering," Lorelei finished.

They were back to fighting mode, and Alex gave Lorelei a sharp look. "If only you knew the joy of success. Right, sister?"

Sarah's vision blurred and shifted as she glanced at her drink, then back at Alex. The lights seemed to dim as she tried to straighten herself in her chair.

Lorelei touched her arm. "You have the most beautiful light."

Sarah met Lorelei's gaze. "You can see it?"

"Of course. So lovely and so much potential."

Alex almost snarled at Lorelei. "Not now."

Sarah's eyes grew heavy as her energy drained away. The scotch had knocked her down. But she had only taken a few sips.

She looked back at Alex. Had he noticed her weakness? She forced herself to sit upright—strong drinks always affected her more than others because of her smaller frame—but the loss of control was embarrassing. If she could just get upstairs to her room... "What we did outside... the door of light must have taken away my strength." She steadied herself in her chair. "Or maybe from the attack..."

"To be expected," Alex said.

Now they were both staring at her. She rubbed her eyes. "I'm sorry."

"Stop being sorry, girl." Lorelei stroked her forearm. "You've made it all worthwhile."

"Made what worthwhile?" Sarah's words slurred together. "Am I drunk?"

"Oh yes, dear. *Very* drunk, and nosey." Lorelei wrapped her hand around Sarah's arm and pulled. "What did you think of my light last night?"

"Your light?"

"I saw yours. You saw mine. I felt you watching me from the doorway. Let me take you to my room and show you some of the things possible with your new expanded gift. Some of the things Alex would never dare show you."

Alex held Sarah's other arm. "You can't destroy the door of light."

Lorelei's grip tightened. "But you can? Like you did to Cecilia?"

Sarah took a sudden breath and froze. What were they saying? The room was getting darker, and it was impossible to keep her eyes open much longer. She leaned toward Alex, although Lorelei still held her arm as they played tug-of-war with her.

"Don't even think about it," Alex told Lorelei.

Sarah tried to stand. She reached out to Alex, clutching his shirt to balance herself. "I need to lie down."

Alex helped to steady her as she moved away from the table, throwing one arm around her waist to prop her up even as Lorelei refused to let go.

"I'm taking her out there," he said.

"And you talk of me destroying her?"

"Out where?" Sarah asked.

Lorelei scoffed. "To his wife and child."

His wife and child? Sarah nearly toppled forward as she struggled out of his arms and stood wavering as she stumbled backwards. "What are you talking about? Your wife and child... they died."

"They did," he said sadly. "Lauren and little Anna passed away. But your light..."

Lorelei laughed while staring into Sarah's eyes. "Understand yet, dummy?" The woman's voice echoed within the fog of Sarah's fading consciousness.

Sarah took another step, then collapsed to the floor. Alex caught her, although her elbow crashed down against the wood surface, sending a jolt of pain up through her shoulder and spine. She turned toward the front door and crawled. Something awful was about to happen. If she could just get outside, maybe she could call for help. She clutched the edge of a rug and used it to pull herself forward.

Lorelei appeared over her and stood in her path. "Not that way."

The voices of Alex and Lorelei blurred together above her, although she made out the words with great difficulty.

"Don't ever tell me I didn't help you," Lorelei said. "If you fry her brain like you did Cecilia's..."

"It won't happen again," Alex said. "She is the real thing."

"At least she's not our damn sister."

A moment later, Lorelei's face hovered within Sarah's vision only inches away. The woman had gotten down on her hands and knees with her fingers curled below her chin like the paws of a cat ready to pounce. "You'll do as Alex says, understand?"

Sarah's mouth gaped as she gasped for breath, and she focused on Lorelei's eyes. Somewhere past the wintry gray and deep within the black of her pupils burned a small white flame.

"It won't kill you..." Lorelei said. "Not quite. But who knows, maybe you and Cecilia will come to be great friends if Alex fails again."

Sarah's vision went dark.

✵ 27 ✵

E mmie and Jason had been at their hotel in St. Augustine for two hours before Finn arrived. Emmie opened the door for him and embraced him without hesitation. "Finn!"

His face was full of anxiety, but it also showed joy and relief upon seeing her and Jason. "I got here as fast as I could. Any news?"

"She still won't answer."

Emmie pulled him inside and led him to a pair of chairs across the room. Sitting on the edge of the bed while the men took the chairs, she started telling him all that she and Jason had learned about Temper House. The family's history, the astral projections, the "angel of death."

After she was done, she said, "Tell us exactly everything Natalia told you."

"She was there seventeen years ago, when she was sixteen. The parents died since, and there are three Temper siblings left in the house now, as far as she knows," Finn said. "The boy was an empath, like Sarah. The older daughter, Lorelei, is meant to be gifted at astral projection. She's supposed to be a wild, difficult woman. Acted like the star pupil at the school, though the parents kept trying to develop the light in her sister, Cecilia, who was only about twelve or so. Natalia also heard that Cecilia was injured in a separate accident more recently. Officially, the young woman had a stroke, although Natalia suggested her siblings might be responsible for what happened to her too."

Emmie pictured the "angel" spirit. "I think the one dealing in astral projection must be the thing we've seen."

"Where?" Finn asked sharply.

"Right after she killed Jason's contact, Howard, at his house. We arrived just after she killed him, but I didn't know who it was until now. It fits. This Lorelei also must've killed Dr. Albright."

"The book that had information on the family was somewhat recent," Jason said, "and it mentioned the Temper parents died in some accident. I've been trying to find out more about this, but no one is talking. Did Natalia know?"

"She knew other students who were around at the time," Finn said. "No one saw it happen, but the rumor was—it wasn't an accident. It involved some sort of confrontation between the Tempers and a group of psychics who were trying to stop their particular studies."

Sitting back, Jason threw Emmie a look. "And how much would you bet that one of the psychics involved in the confrontation was Dr. Albright? He must've tried to stop them from doing something that endangered everyone. That's what Howard meant when he said, 'They dared...' The kids dared to keep developing the astral projection thing and the angel of death. And now they took their revenge on Dr. Albright and Howard, and maybe others will be next."

"They left the rose as a signature to their revenge, then," Finn said. He looked white under his tan. "That means they're not afraid."

Jason also seemed spooked. "Means they developed this thing until they think they can face the big fish."

"We have to do something about it." Emmie shot to her feet and began to pace. "Also, it has to be more than just revenge." She looked at Finn. "You said Natalia spoke of the door of light."

"She said they were obsessed with the idea. Must be why they wanted Sarah, because of Whisper House," Finn said. "I just don't know how the Temper family knew about her, how they got to her, especially without us knowing about it."

Jason cleared his throat. They looked at him; he was staring at the floor. "I'm not *positive* about this, but I *did* mention to a couple of friends that Sarah had become beautiful light."

Finn scowled at him. "So it was you and your big mouth."

"I didn't mean to cause any problems."

"You knew it was a big deal, otherwise why mention it at all?"

"It just sort of slipped out during normal conversation between people like me. Like us."

"People of Carey Kali, you mean," Emmie said severely. "You know better than to blab about something like this if it involves us."

"It escaped. I never thought—"

Finn leaned toward Jason, his hands curled into fists. "Why would you talk about Sarah like that? Were you trying to impress someone? Trying to schmooze your way into some big business deal?"

Jason held his palms out as he leaned back. "Nothing like that, I swear."

"If anything happens to her..."

"They need her well and whole. You can count on that. There's no way anyone would harm the door of light, apparently, if that's what she is."

"You know that's exactly what she is."

"And so she is the most coveted—"

"Thing?" Finn bent to meet Jason's elusive gaze with a piercing stare of his own. "You're talking about her like she's merchandise."

Jason swallowed. "Listen, kick my ass later. We need to get Sarah out of there. I think we can all agree on that."

Emmie touched Finn's shoulder. "It's true. And we won't leave here without her, I promise."

Squeezing the black stone on his necklace with a solemn face, Finn inched back.

Emmie checked her phone. Sarah hadn't contacted her for too long now.

"If they had a purpose for her, they might've taken away her phone." Finn watched her. "I say we storm the place."

"Not the best idea," Emmie said. "You haven't seen the angel —or devil—of light like we did. There was crazy power behind that spirit, and we saw firsthand what it can do." She flipped through the photos on her phone and stopped at one, holding it out to Finn. The photo she had taken of Howard's body. "*That's* what happens to someone who messes with that family."

Finn stared at the photo for several seconds, then looked away. "It just makes me want to go in there *now*."

"Well, Finn, you're not a great strategist kind of because of that," Emmie said. "We need to think about this."

"We could show up at the door like random tourists," Jason said, "and ask to see the zoo. You read about the zoo, Finn? Lots of tourists in the St. Augustine area. It wouldn't seem out of place to stop by and act curious and clueless."

"But the angel of death, which might be Lorelei, got a good look at us. It saw our faces." Emmie gestured to herself and Jason. "It would recognize us."

"I'll go," Finn said. "Natalia told me about the zoo, and I did some digging on the way. It isn't public knowledge, not on any tourist website, but it was open way back in the day. Wealthy houses used to let people come over for arranged visits then. Nothing stops me from acting like I still believe they offer tours. Maybe I can just get Sarah's attention long enough to coax her out of the house. It's our only shot."

Emmie nodded slowly. "We'll stay back at the car, out of sight, and you just make a run for it at the first sign of trouble, got it?"

"Don't worry. I'm not afraid."

"That's what I'm afraid of. Just don't take any unnecessary

risks. Get in the house, if you can, and we'll be waiting for your return." Emmie looked up and down at Finn. His tanned skin would help with the charade. "It could work."

"In case we need to escape, we need a map—the place is apparently huge and surrounded by a swamp," Finn said. "Satellite maps to the rescue."

28

Finn stepped up to the video doorbell attached to a silver box on a gray painted pole beside the main gate leading into Temper House. Through the metal bars he gazed at the windows first, wondering if they had already seen him approaching. He pushed a thought into the window's darkness. *Sarah, are you in there? We'll get you out soon, I promise.* Maybe she would catch his thoughts, even if he couldn't receive hers.

He pressed the video doorbell button, and it sprang to life only a moment later. A man's cautious voice asked, "Can I help you?"

Finn cleared his throat. "Yes, I'm from out of town and I read about the zoo you have behind your property. Can I talk to someone about that?"

"I'm sorry, but what about it?"

"Uh—I read some articles about the history of the place. Saw some images in a book, and it seems like something so unique. I'm wondering if you had a minute to let me have a look?"

"It's not open to the public."

"I know. I should have called," Finn insisted. "But I'm also a journalist. Sometimes I discover these things on the fly and—"

"I'll be right down," the man said abruptly.

The gate screeched and clattered open, and he stepped onto the property, following a sidewalk to the front door. Emmie and Jason were waiting for him back at the car, only half a block away, and they had warned him not to take any chances—but he had no plans to leave there without Sarah. Even if he couldn't get in through the front door, he would risk anything to get her out.

Arriving at the front door, he touched his necklace again to remind himself not to be a kamikaze just for the sake of it. Better not make it a habit to be touching that stone every ten minutes either, but he let it drop over his long-sleeved shirt. He had such destructive habits that he did need some sort of reminder to keep him from returning to them.

The Circe of Cuba had not just handed him a metaphor: she had made a literal touchstone for him.

Something moved in the brush just beyond the edge of the house, and one glassy eye peered out between blades of grass. The thing, however, was well camouflaged and too far away for him to identify it. The sunlight reflected off its dull, furless skin, but judging by the outline of its body within the shadows, it looked a little larger than a crouching dog.

The thing shifted closer. Its proximity unnerved him. It could get to him in a matter of seconds, if it wanted, but even the threat of some wild animal couldn't rip him away from that doorway. He took a deep breath and pulled himself together.

Finn took that moment to glance through the small opaque window beside the door. Faint scattered light passed through the foggy glass and a shadow moved. He tensed as footsteps approached, and someone on the other side unlocked the dead-bolt and opened the door.

A young, fair-haired man eyed him curiously. "It's been a long time since anyone asked to look at the zoo."

"I can imagine. Sorry to insist, but I haven't come across anything quite like that."

The man's gaze dropped to the necklace around Finn's neck, then down to his pockets and back up to his face. He stared into

Finn's eyes for several seconds before answering. The man pushed the door wide open. "I can give you a quick tour. What's your name?"

"Finn Adams. I've seen pictures of the statues and structures. They looked like palaces to Hindu gods."

The man's face relaxed and brightened. "You know your art history." He held out his hand. "I'm Alex Temper."

Finn shook it. Alex gestured for him to step inside. "Please, come in."

As he walked into the house, Finn's senses heightened. A rush of cool air swept in as Alex shut the door behind him. A row of light jackets and heavier coats hung in a neat line in the entryway. Finn recognized a red wine-colored coat immediately. Sarah's. His heart quickened. She was there.

Alex led him away from the front door. "It's funny you should stop by today. I was just telling my sister it feels selfish to have it and never show it. That's how my great-great-grandfather felt, anyway, but today's world is a bit trickier. A lot more tourism, for one."

"Well, it must be a lot of work to maintain something like that. But he had a point." Finn spoke louder than he normally would have, almost to the point of shouting. He glanced into every doorway he passed as Alex took him deeper into the house.

A young woman's voice echoed from somewhere upstairs, but it wasn't Sarah's. One of the sisters? The voice sang in a melodic repetition, soft and sweet yet full of sadness. He couldn't make out the words.

"How far did you travel to get here?" Alex asked.

"Not far. I'm traveling through Florida on vacation." Finn threw his voice in every direction as he walked to announce his presence. If Sarah heard him, she might come running out of one of the rooms.

They turned a corner and he peeked into a darkened library. Nothing. Alex Temper led him to the back porch and paused as they stared out over the backyard toward the zoo. No sign of Sarah, but he would follow through with his tour of the zoo. *Maybe she'll see me walking around.* The more time on the property, the better chance he would have of finding her.

They headed out through the garden and into the zoo area, which was lined by a stone wall. They passed two large ornate cages that resembled small shrines to giant gods.

"Brahma and Vishnu," Finn said, inspecting the illustrations painted along the edges.

"You also know your Hindu gods."

"I've traveled to India four times."

"It's good to have a diverse knowledge of cultures." Alex stopped near the zoo's entrance and glanced down at Finn's necklace again. "That, for example, is interesting."

Finn touched it. "Yeah, a cultural souvenir, you could say."

"Where from?" Alex crossed his arms over his chest.

Finn hesitated. He scrambled to get his facts straight to lie but gave up. "I don't remember."

"A Cuban woman, by any chance?"

Finn's breath paused.

"She's quite attractive, don't you think?" Alex insisted.

"Who? I don't even remember if it was a woman."

"How can you forget someone like Natalia?" Alex reached out and touched the stone at the end of the necklace, pulling on it for a moment before releasing it. "Her craftsmanship is distinctive, and at first I thought maybe she had sent you here to spy on me." Alex stared into Finn's eyes. "But then, after I saw you at the door, I remembered your face..."

"What do you mean?"

Alex's smile faded. "You can't move."

"Excuse me?" A strange sensation swept through Finn's body.

"You're going to stay right there and do everything I say."

"What are you talking about?" Finn tried to move back but his legs and body had stopped reacting to him. A nauseous anxiety filled his chest. What was happening? Dark magic? It was like the Hydes all over again. Before his arms stiffened, he managed to reach up and touch the stone on the necklace. He tried to focus on what Natalia had instructed him to do with it, but his mind had become blank.

As Finn held the stone between his fingers, Alex sneered. "It's worthless, you know. Didn't she tell you? Just a souvenir, but I can't deny that she is skilled at cutting them. Obsidian stone is like cutting a diamond, you know. All hand-carved and each one unique."

Finn's heart raced and he shouted, "Sarah!"

"Quiet," Alex commanded.

Finn's voice cut out. How could his voice obey Alex Temper's command? This was the big league he had mentioned to Natalia. It was exactly what he had feared: to become powerless before one of these people again. Finn tried to call out Sarah's name again but only air escaped his throat.

"What a wonderful opportunity to have you visit on this special day for Temper House. Serendipity at its finest. You don't need to struggle or sneak around or fight me."

Finn tried to reach out and grab Alex by the neck, but his arms floundered and missed their target. It was as if he were a puppet, and more so when Alex stepped toward the zoo, saying, "Follow me."

There was no way to resist. Finn's limbs moved independently as he strained with every ounce of energy to escape whatever had come over him.

This isn't supposed to happen. God, bronze star my ass. I suck!

Alex led Finn along past the garden and out toward a large stone building in the center of the zoo. A central dome rose above the other structures around it, with a complexity to its design that mirrored the other Hindu themes of the zoo. Bright colors and gold leaf accented the exotic designs at the entrance, where a tall gateway to the main door stood, with a series of smaller arches beside it.

"There were some photos on her dresser, and I couldn't resist taking a look at them. The two of you looked so happy embracing. That kind of love is rare and worth fighting for. So I have no intention of harming either of you. Quite the contrary. This is a rare chance for you to witness one of the most important moments in psychic history. And it all came about because the woman you love trained here. She's remarkable; you'll see."

The guy was beginning to look a little crazy; Finn was used to searching for that sting of lunacy some people had. It was in Alex Temper's eyes. He drew comfort from the fact that Alex apparently needed Sarah "well and whole," from what Jason had said.

Opening the door to the structure, Alex stepped inside with Finn.

The walls were adorned with intricate carvings depicting scenes from Hindu mythology. Candlelight revealed a stage and a central altar. Flowers were stacked beside two stone structures a little larger than coffins. A nearby table displayed framed photos of a woman and a young girl.

A mausoleum.

Alex led Finn back a few steps and positioned him in a darkened corner beside the door. He was almost out of sight behind the statue of a god, four-armed and fanged Yama. The god of death and justice held a noose, wherein he would catch the souls of those about to die.

From behind the statue of Yama, Finn could see the whole space. And yet he might not be seen if Sarah came. And he still couldn't move.

"You'll wait here." Alex paused in the doorway. "I won't be gone long, and I have a surprise for you when I get back. I think you know what it is."

A silent scream thickened Finn's throat as Alex left and the door clicked shut behind him.

❧ 29 ❧

Sarah woke up with Alex standing over her. Whatever had clouded her mind now faded as reality returned. She sat up suddenly and clutched at the sheet covering most of her body. "Where am I?"

Alex gestured for her to stay down. "Take it easy. Don't stand up too quickly. You might hurt yourself."

She was sitting on her bed and still fully dressed. The setting sun warmed the room with an orange glow. Her head ached, and a pressure pushed against the back of her eyes—a pain she hadn't felt since her party days in college. A hangover. She struggled to remember what she'd been doing before this. Had she really gotten drunk? Impossible. What had she been drinking?

Scotch. She had sipped a glass in the kitchen with... Lorelei.

And the rest was foggy. But Sarah had wanted to run.

Alex stood beside her with a gentle smile, as usual. "Everything's going to be just fine."

She tried to stand again, but lost her balance. "What did you do to me?"

"I'm sorry. My sister tends to overreact. She wanted to make sure you wouldn't try to leave."

"I didn't want to leave, but I do now. She drugged me."

"She showed restraint, actually. But Lorelei isn't stupid. She values you as much as I do."

"Strange way of showing it."

He stared into her eyes with curiosity. "After I explain the situation, I'm sure that you'll understand. But I think it's best we take a walk so I can do it properly."

His face was gentle, and his eyes held the same soft glow that she had trusted and admired only hours earlier, but now all that had taken a sinister turn. He kept his distance, although he stood between her and the door. She glanced around for her phone.

"Your phone is safe. You'll get it back, I promise, just after we complete the process."

"What process?"

"Please..." The pleading eyes boring into her were like those of her desperately sick hospital patients. "I need your help. And you're the only one who can help me."

Sarah rubbed her forehead. The pain had subsided a little. "I remember Lorelei said something about Cecilia, and that you had failed."

"I'll never forgive myself for what's happened to her." He frowned and stared at the floor, then brightened. "But we can still extract a great deal of joy from that tragedy if you'll follow me."

"What did you do to her?" Her memory returned slowly. "You used her for something... Her gifts?"

He took a step back and offered his hand.

"Come to the garden. I'm sure that your heart will understand after I show you."

She sensed the honesty in his words and the almost imperceptible colors of his aura emanating in a steady flow of greens and blues. Colors of truth. She didn't take his hand, but she got to her feet. "I'm trusting you."

He seemed pleased. "Thank you, Sarah."

Sarah's mind still reeled from the effects of the alcohol or whatever drug Lorelei had put into it. She steadied herself as Alex took her arm and led her downstairs and outside through the back door. The garden was alive with a small flock of birds that had perched in the trees near the zoo. They were singing all around them while the wind rustled the branches and leaves. The air was a little cooler and dry.

Sarah found she could stand unaided, although she strained to focus on the reality of her surroundings. They passed the location where she had trained earlier, and she tensed near the place where the bobcat had nearly attacked her, wondering if something else might emerge from the shadows to finish her off.

They walked toward the zoo and followed the winding brick path past several of the large ornate cages. The noises from the animals erupted as she walked by, but Alex seemed not to notice.

He gestured to the taller pavilion she hadn't explored yet. "There."

"What's in there?" She slowed.

"You're afraid of me now," he told her quietly. "I feel your fear, but I won't hurt you—*nobody* will hurt you here, not even a little bit. We have a deep reverence for you."

Glancing back toward the house, Sarah found the porch empty. But she sensed a familiar energy nearby, except that it was somehow cut off. "Who's in there?"

Alex didn't answer.

A sense of unease passed through her. "Is someone dying?"

"You'll understand soon."

They arrived at the entrance to the elaborately constructed structure and Alex held the door open although she didn't step inside. The smell of something burning passed through the air. *Candles? Incense?*

Stepping through the open door with Alex at her side, she spotted a massive wall of granite squares against the far side of the room. Each square was roughly two feet across, and names and dates were carved into each one. A memorial? Two squares were open and empty, and the granite slabs that would seal the opening sat on the ground just below the openings.

A mausoleum.

Fresh flowers adorned two stone caskets that sat below an altar at the front of the room. The altar was covered with a white cloth and held two large framed portraits.

A woman and a young girl. Alex's wife and daughter. Their names were printed beneath their photos. Lauren and Anna.

Sarah stood petrified as dozens of candles burned around the area, providing enough light for her to see everything clearly even after Alex closed the door.

Lorelei's words came back to her now. *Understand yet, dummy?*

No. No, she didn't want to understand. It was too horrible.

"Alex, what's all this?"

"It's everything I wanted you to see and know." He pointed at the portraits. "My wife and daughter. I told you they died a year ago."

She looked away from the stone coffins. "Do you think I'm a medium? I'm not skilled at talking with the dead."

"That's not why you're here. Stop pretending you don't know, Sarah."

Alex *had* mentioned Whisper House, she now realized. By name. And she was sure she hadn't ever told him the name of the house.

"All this—you went looking for me on purpose. Because you thought I was the door of light, which might—" She stopped short, her chest heaving. She didn't want to say it, not in that place where he seemed to expect—

"Not *might,* Sarah." His cheeks flushed. *"Will.* The door of light *will* bring them back."

Sarah turned to run, but he held her back.

"But they died naturally, didn't they?" She pulled her arm away. It was all a nightmare. It had to be.

"Yes. The virus took them."

"They can't come back. Don't you see? They've already moved on."

"That's only what we've been told."

"It's not just a theory. That's how dying works. It's impossible for a spirit to come back after they've passed into the light."

Alex's expression became somber. "In the natural order of things."

"What do you mean?"

"I mean that nobody can do what you can do. You can make yourself the doorway of light again, just like you did in the garden, and they will return to me."

Sarah paused her breathing. Her swirling mind struggled to grasp the words. "The animals... your abominations. And Cecilia... You forced her to bring back animals for you because you thought she was the door of light. And she brought back things that were rotten, didn't she? What did you do, Alex? You demanded so much that you fried her mind, like Lorelei said?"

"She couldn't do it," he said sharply. "But you can. You can become the door of light again and bring Lauren and little Anna back just like you did with the rabbit. The rabbit was perfect! And the spirits of my wife and child aren't that far away. We are never that far away from our loved ones. It's just a thin veil that separates us, a door that you can open. It's that simple."

Now she looked toward the caskets. "The rabbit had only died hours before that. No time for..." Her sensitivity prevented her from saying the last word.

"Decay?" Tears flowed from Alex's eyes. "With love, all things are possible. Don't you know that?"

"This isn't about love. It's another abomination!"

"It's all about love. You know that firsthand, as you took the love my sister felt for her rabbit, her longing, and transformed it into light, and that became life." He took a step in her direction, and she had never seen his gray eyes look so intense. They seemed like blades. "I mean quite literally that love can do this. Through you."

Again, Sarah shook her head. "Whatever we did out there with that rabbit, that was just a fluke. I was pushing myself to my limits then and it barely even worked."

"It wasn't a fluke. It was perfect. I need you to do that same thing again, although on a larger scale. Open that door of light again, take my love for them, and I'll be right here with you to lead my wife and little girl back to me. It won't take long."

"Physical matter breaks down. They wouldn't be the same in any way, even if I was able to bring them back. Have you seen the animals? Alex, are you mad?"

"They were taken from me. My girl was robbed from my arms by a virus and I never even got to say goodbye."

"It's the order of things," she said softly, now touching his arms. "It hurts. I know it does, but you have to accept it."

More tears spilled from his eyes. "Your door can reverse the order and bring them back. I know you can. You know it."

"No."

He looked at her with something like regret for a second. "It hurts that you'd deny me, Sarah. I've come to truly care for you. But this is the only thing that matters to me, so I'll need to show you how it feels." Alex nodded slowly while stepping over to the darkened side of the room. He pulled someone from behind a large statue as if leading a blind person.

Sarah immediately recognized the young man.

Finn.

A wave of panic, horror, and joy swept through her as she rushed past Alex and embraced Finn. Tears flowed down her cheeks now. He wasn't moving or responding to her embrace. "What have you done to him?"

"He's alive and well. And everyone will go home *alive* soon."

Sarah checked Finn's pulse and pupils for signs of trauma. He was alive and stable, but his skin was cold and his muscles were solid, as if stuck in a constant state of hypertension. Only his eyes swung in lazy arcs that followed Sarah as she moved around him. "You can't leave him like this. Release him from whatever you've done or I won't do a thing for you. Not a *thing*."

"I won't leave him like that, but don't you see his presence means something? His love for you is strong, like the beacon of light you have inside you. He felt you might need him, and he came. You need to understand that love never gives up. It's destiny pointing the way for you, showing you through Finn what love means and how much it can hurt when you lose it."

Sarah faced Alex. "Let him go."

"I promise you will both leave here alive. I'm not a monster, Sarah. You must know that."

"Finn, I'm so sorry. I'll get you out of here." Sarah kissed Finn's cheek. She tasted the cool, salty sweat on his skin as it mixed with her own tears.

"Do you see how you feel? And he's right here, alive. Imagine me losing my wife. My child. And you can help me, just as I can help you by letting him go."

A deep rage swept through her as she turned back to Alex. "What kind of empath are you? It's impossible for an empath to destroy a sister, to pretend friendship and trick someone, to threaten someone with a person she loves!" She got close to him, peering into his face. "What are you, really, Alex?"

"Traveler," he said in a low voice. "It's how my parents called it. Lorelei too. I guess we were all wrong about Cecilia. She was probably an empath, and that's why—"

"That's why she kept doing as you asked, drinking in your pain, until it destroyed her."

Alex didn't bother to stop the torrent of tears that kept falling from his eyes. His face and neck, and the collar of his shirt, were soaking wet. "I love my sister. I adore her." His eyes found Sarah's again. "But a child... Nothing comes before your child. Nothing in the world. I should have kept her safe. She should have lived."

There it was, that pull she always felt to comfort those in pain. Alex stood as if on a scaffold, showing his pain. It was a river of endless grief. Such a great part of her wanted to comfort him, knowing that he was a good man—or had been.

But she wouldn't take the bait. He would know how to manipulate that, and she must keep a cool head. For one, she must get Finn out of there, at whatever cost.

"After I'm done becoming the door of light for you," she said, unable to keep her voice from quivering, "I'm walking out that door with him or I will make your life a nightmare. I'll push your family's spirits back into the light forever."

With a sob of joy, Alex stepped toward the caskets. "You couldn't become an extractor, not you. And there's no need for threats. I intend to keep my promises."

Sarah trembled as she tried to focus on what she needed to do. Her face warmed and a toxic anger burned in her chest. There was no way out of it.

She walked over to the two closed caskets with Alex watching her every move and stared into the eyes of the woman and child in the photos. A little girl who looked so much like Alex, and a woman with soft brown eyes and a pretty, kind face. They must have been happy...

"If this doesn't work, I'm taking Finn out of here either way."

"It will work," Alex said. "Don't doubt it. I'll be right there with you."

I'll be right there with you.

Nothing meant to comfort her. A warning. He would be with her and would know if she backed away on purpose and pretended not to manage it. She touched the edge of Lauren's casket first, and the cold surface chilled her fingertips. Sarah closed her eyes and focused on the same healing energy that she had formed to heal the rabbit earlier. The beaming light swelled within her mind and encompassed her body in just minutes. She couldn't see it with eyes shut; this time, she just knew.

Alex pushed open the lids of the coffins while she continued drawing in the light, opening her eyes a bit as a pungent odor of decomposition rose around her and threatened to derail her concentration. She cringed, turning her face away slightly, but continued.

The love was there. An overwhelming, emotional energy that streamed from Alex's pained heart and radiated toward the bodies like a powerful spotlight. The cascading waves of light and warmth passed through Sarah. She held the light and magnified it with a crippling intensity that brought her to the brink of fainting.

The light grew brighter and surrounded her like a cocoon of energy. It blinded her senses as it expanded, brighter than it had ever been, heating to an uncomfortable degree as she sensed the light opening above her. The presence of Lauren and Anna appeared on the other side. They had come from so far away. A timeless space beyond. And now they moved through the door of light that she had somehow created between their two worlds.

Cries of joy erupted from Alex as the flowing wisps of spirits merged with the bodies until two choking gasps of air broke the silence.

Sarah collapsed.

30

It was taking Finn far too long to return. Emmie checked her phone. He'd been gone for over an hour, and her anxiety became unbearable.

"We can't wait anymore," Emmie said.

Jason nodded. "I don't have a good feeling about it either."

They hurried onto the property a moment later. Using the satellite maps to avoid the swamp and the zoo, they climbed over a section of metal fence, where a sagging tree branch and crumbling mortar between some bricks provided an awkward stepladder to the top. On the other side, they hid within the shadows and paused for a moment to get their bearings.

"It's as if the house had swallowed them up." Jason stared at a shaded window above them.

Emmie followed his gaze without answering, then led him around toward the back of the house. They spotted the garden and the edge of the zoo they'd seen from the satellite map.

Jason nodded toward the zoo. "Impressive."

Emmie nodded and took it all in. What statues she could see were elaborate and interesting, and the structures beyond them made her feel as if she'd stepped into another time and place. Under different circumstances, she would have loved to walk among those grand designs and marveled at their construction, but her friends were prisoners of the place. "Could they have gone back there?"

Jason glanced toward the house. "Could have."

The idea of Sarah and Finn trapped near the animals—or *with* the animals—made her stomach churn. Her impatience surged. "On that vast property, they could be *anywhere*."

"I hear something," Jason said.

Emmie tuned her attention toward the noise too. A woman's voice, and it was coming from somewhere above them. She peeked her head around the corner, trying to view the source, and spotted an open window on the second floor. A young woman's face appeared in the window, and she looked out over the backyard, singing some strange melody that held no rhythm. Her voice was sweet and pleasant, but Emmie could not make out the words from that distance.

Emmie pulled back. "There's someone up there. She might see us."

The voice stopped suddenly.

Emmie held still, listening for a minute before she peered around the corner again. The upstairs window slammed shut and Emmie shuddered.

Jason rested his hand on her back. "Did she see you?"

"I don't think so. But it wasn't Sarah." Emmie didn't waste any time. She made a stealthy dash toward the back porch. Jason followed her. If the woman was upstairs, then maybe someone else was also up there. That moment would be their best shot at getting inside unnoticed.

She arrived at the porch with Jason and moved across to the back door. The floor creaked as they crept forward, even as she carefully shifted her weight with each step. Emmie touched the door handle and glanced back at Jason. He gave a reassuring nod, and she turned it.

It was unlocked. She pushed it open with great care and entered the silent house.

It wasn't difficult to see inside. Many of the lights were on, but they had no idea which way to go. They moved slowly into the back area. A long hallway stretched ahead of them and there were doors on either side. One of the doors was open, revealing a library inside. Photos and artwork covered the walls as they stepped in further and closed the door behind them, shutting out the cold air.

Emmie's ears perked at every sound, although there were no voices coming from anywhere now, not even from the woman upstairs. She peeked around every corner, moving stealthily as her body tensed, preparing to run at any moment, and Jason was just as quick and quiet. She had already decided that if someone discovered them or the angel of death appeared, she would scream Sarah's and Finn's name as loudly as she could and race through the house. No sense in dialing the police. Bullets wouldn't work to stop a spirit.

They made it as far as the stairway near the entrance when a door opened upstairs and someone stepped out into the hallway. There wasn't anything they could do except move back. Slipping into a darkened room with a single lamp switched on in the corner, they stood quietly out of sight.

Emmie took the moment to scan their surroundings. The walls were adorned with framed photos showing the history of the exotic Temper zoo. It was a sort of shrine to the way things had been at the house decades earlier. An antique oak roll-top desk sat in the corner surrounded by Hindu-themed statues and artwork.

The person upstairs was coming down, although not taking steps. There were scraping noises and heavy gasps for air at each stride, as if the person were carefully *sliding* down. A woman's soft voice rose above the thumps and scuffle. It was the same voice Emmie had heard from the open window.

Jason pulled Emmie back further as the woman moved down the stairs, but Emmie resisted. Something was strangely alluring about the woman's voice and movements.

The woman chanted as she descended the stairs, "Love is patient, love is kind, Little Bo Peep has lost her mind..."

Emmie poked her head out of the room and leaned forward to get a glimpse of the figure through the stair railings. The woman wasn't standing. She was sliding along the stairs, walking with her arms and one twisted leg bent beneath her at an odd angle. The woman glanced around as she descended, but she didn't seem to notice Emmie or Jason.

They were trapped there. Emmie glanced down the hallway toward the back door. They could run, but she wasn't leaving without her friends. Inside the room again, they waited silently as the woman reached the bottom of the stairs and turned toward them, her frazzled blonde hair hiding her face.

They stepped further into the shadows and kept still, hoping they hadn't accidentally wandered into the woman's destination. Emmie held her breath as the woman paused in the doorway and, clutching the door's frame with both hands to steady herself, she turned and stared right at her. Emmie caught a glimpse of her face and eyes.

Had she seen them?

Emmie prepared to carry out her plan to scream, but there was something childlike in the woman's expression. An amusing grin passed over her face. "Hide and go seek..." she mumbled.

Emmie took a deep breath, ready to scream Sarah's and Finn's names. No way out of it. They were caught.

Before she could act, the woman turned away and continued past them, dragging herself along with great difficulty toward the back door without another word.

Jason's confused and startled expression mirrored her own. She had expected a confrontation, but without pausing to question their luck, after the woman was out of sight, Emmie returned to the hallway and prepared to make a stealthy charge up the stairs.

Just outside the room, she stopped suddenly as if paralyzed. An apparition materialized only a few feet away at the bottom of the stairs. The energy bristled in the air like a faint white light and hovered as it expanded, transforming into a woman's intense spirit. The woman's harsh light was blinding, but unmistakable: it belonged to the same angel of death that had taken Howard's life, and now it inched toward her.

❧ 31 ❧

A sinking feeling swept through Finn's chest. This wasn't supposed to happen. Natalia had told him the way to prevent any psychic influences from affecting him. He flexed and strained against the invisible chains that prevented him from lunging at the bastard who had somehow manipulated Sarah into going there to do something insane.

Are you surprised? You didn't complete your training.

Sarah had regained consciousness and was kneeling over the open caskets, trembling as if an electrical current surged through her. Her eyes were closed and her skin was turning red, as if she'd stepped too close to the sun without protection.

Sounds of gasping and choking came from the caskets and echoed throughout the room. Even without being able to move, Finn cringed in disbelief and horror as the repulsive noises grew louder. It wasn't possible. The dead couldn't return.

Alex hovered over the caskets with his hands together as if praying for a miracle, his face at the edge of tears.

Finn raged in his fruitless attempts to charge forward and stop the horror unfolding in front of him. He couldn't look away or close his eyes as Alex reached in and caressed the faces of both the woman and the little girl as they convulsed and came alive.

He wanted to scream, but his dry throat refused to obey.

I'm no better now than I was before.

Staring at Sarah, he focused on the vision of her as she had appeared at Natalia's house. The archetype of an angel. He focused on that soothing image as Sarah continued to follow Alex's instructions.

Sarah's eyes cracked open. Even from that distance, Finn saw a glint of light reflecting in them. And that sparkle of light fired something deep inside him, a connection between them that calmed him. Holding that moment in his mind was all he could do to keep from surrendering to a wave of dark thoughts.

Natalia's words came back to him: *Dark magic cannot enter a mind full of light and joy.*

Alex leaned over to pick up his daughter first, lifting her from the casket as if cradling a baby. The little girl's limbs were limp, and her dried clothing rustled as she rose. Her fingers twitched, her face turning up toward her father, although whatever psychic magic had brought the girl to life had not completely restored her. The sunken, rotting flesh of her cheeks stretched back so that her teeth were fixed in a permanent grin. Her dull, hazy eyes stared straight ahead without shifting, and the muscles in her neck and arms spasmed as Alex pulled the girl into his chest.

"Ah, Anna! My little girl. You've come back," Alex said, the tears still falling. "I missed you so much." He turned toward his wife. "Lauren. Sweetheart! You've come back to me!"

Have you taken a look at them, lunatic? Or are the tears blinding you?

The wife clutched the edge of the coffin with one hand and shuddered as her other hand grabbed the other side. She pulled herself to a sitting position before turning sideways to face Sarah. The dead woman gazed at Sarah, then around the room like a curious newborn witnessing life for the first time. She struggled to get out of the casket even as Alex reached for her, encouraging her to join him. Sarah remained kneeling beside the caskets through the resurrection, seemingly resigned to see it through to the end.

Finn tensed, losing sight of the angelic vision of Sarah for a moment as the panic swept in again.

Get out of there, Sarah! Finn screamed in his mind.

Alex cradled the girl in his arms. Anna's hair was still groomed, hairband matching the tiny, pretty white dress they'd buried her in, but her skin and muscles had darkened and rotted, despite whatever magic had brought her back to life. Her muscles ceaselessly twitched and strained in a chaotic rhythm.

Sarah finally lifted her hand toward Alex. "Alex, look at her!"

Alex seemed not to notice. He swayed with the girl in his arms. "Anna, my sweet baby girl."

"I can't continue," Sarah said with exasperation. "It won't work."

Alex shook his head. "It's already done."

The wife staggered and rose to her feet, hunched forward, and reached toward her daughter as she screamed. Her voice cracked with her guttural cries, hissing and gurgling from a well of decay.

Lovingly placing the girl on the floor near Sarah, Alex propped her into a seated position as if she were a doll, running his fingers through her hair like he had no doubt done so many times in life. The girl's skin stretched and shifted under Alex's touch. Her small jaw opened, gasping in another breath before exhaling a scream.

The ghastly shriek chilled Finn, breaking him further away from his focus on Sarah. Nothing seemed to get her out of the process that Alex had forced her into. Finn couldn't will her to look at him.

The girl slumped to the side and shuddered on the floor like a fish out of water, gasping for more air and clawing at her own skin as if trying to free herself from her thin shell. Pieces of her flesh tore away, slipping off and revealing the bare bones beneath it. Alex forced away the girl's hands, but her tiny frame only seemed to gyrate faster with more energy. She tore away the pieces faster than Alex could stop her.

"No!" Alex grabbed each fallen piece of flesh and desperately tried to piece them back into the place where they belonged. He glared at Sarah. "Do something. Heal my Anna before she kills herself."

"I said it won't work," Sarah said, her voice hoarse. "It's too late. It was unnatural."

"You do something!" Alex screamed at her. "This *is* natural. This is my daughter! A little girl's life."

Lauren had crawled over and toppled to the floor beside the fallen girl, her flesh no better than her child's as she ran her fingers over Anna's face and arms while staring ahead into empty space. She wailed as she touched Anna and dipped her head forward, letting out a mournful cry.

Alex pulled the girl away from her and pleadingly yelled into the girl's face, "Wake up, Anna! Don't you quit on me." Alex stood and pressed the side of his face to his child's chest, even as the girl continued to scream, then sat up, straightened his arms and pressed his hands against the girl's heart as if to give her CPR. Alex thrust his arms down into her rib cage. Bones cracked under the weight, and a hiss of air escaped Anna's throat.

The girl stopped screaming.

Alex trembled while turning to Sarah. "Heal her!"

"It's too late. Her spirit is gone."

Alex shook his head. "You're lying. Do it!"

His wife still screamed as she grabbed Alex's forearm, pulling him down toward her. Within the twitching mesh of rotting muscles, her pained expression was mixed with rage.

Alex scooped up the girl and thrust her toward Sarah. "Bring her back."

"It doesn't work that way." Sarah's shoulders drooped. "The door is closed."

"Then open it again."

The mother wobbled as she stood and clutched the girl in Alex's arms. She ran her hands across the girl's chest and face and then grabbed Alex's arms, following them to his shoulders and stopping at his neck. He lurched backward, but she had already dug her fingers into his skin. Blood streamed down his chest and washed over the girl's white dress. Alex tripped on a vase of daisies beside the casket, and all three of them tumbled. Their bodies thumped to the ground together, the wife's gurgling voice rising as Alex cried out in pain. She dug her fingers deeper into his flesh, ripping away at his muscles and pulling at his bones as blood streamed over the floor.

Finn couldn't look away, although he tried. The scene would haunt his nightmares for the rest of his life.

Alex wrestled his way out from under his wife, reaching toward Sarah with wide, glossy eyes, his mouth straining in a silent scream, but he collapsed moments later in a pool of blood.

Sarah solemnly bent forward as if mourning the gruesome deaths.

Yet the mother still moved, crawling to the girl and sweeping her arms under the twice-lifeless corpse, pulling her child up to her chest before curling beside her and wilting as if slipping into a deep sleep. Her body stiffened, and silence filled the air.

Finally, Sarah turned toward Finn. Her eyes still sparkled, and something settled over him like a warm blanket. He stared into her eyes as the light seemed to pass between them. The darkness Alex had conjured still held him in place, but he allowed that spark of light from Sarah's eyes to fill his mind.

Natalia's words again came back to him: *Shadows can't hide when the sun shines in every direction.*

The sparkle in Sarah's eyes swept through him like an angelic love releasing him from all fear.

That was what Natalia had meant.

As if freed from a block of ice, he stepped toward Sarah. Then he ran to her.

❧ 32 ❧

The apparition appeared only a few feet away, and the blazing being shone brighter as Emmie focused on it. Its searing intensity warmed her face and hands as if she were facing the sun. It was the same angel of death she had seen at Howard's house. Its white-hot form was more defined, and the burning light was piercing as she drew away from it.

She now knew this was Lorelei. The oldest Temper child.

But it moved with her even as she stumbled backwards toward the back door.

Jason came up beside her, shielding his eyes, and pulled at her arm. "Em."

"Yeah, I hoped this wouldn't be here too..."

Emmie stopped to face it.

The spirit paused with her, and through the shifting waves of light, Lorelei's expression shifted to amusement. "I always knew we would meet again. But you've gone and saved me a trip. Astral projection is rather tiring, I must admit."

"Where is she?" Emmie demanded.

Lorelei's face faded in and out of the harsh light, but in the absence of details her piercing eyes stood out and focused on

Emmie until they jumped to Jason. "And you've brought your friend. I couldn't be more delighted."

"Where is Sarah?" Emmie repeated.

"Your friend is off playing with my brother in the backyard. Does that scare you?"

"No more than you do."

Lorelei's expression lightened. "So brave! But you wouldn't have come here to rescue her if you thought she wasn't in trouble. My brother killed two birds with one stone. Imagine that. He finally did something right."

Emmie focused on a thin wisp of energy running off behind the spirit like a tail. It swept through the air, nearly imperceptible, like a winding cord of light, and she followed it with her eyes as it led somewhere upstairs. "If you hurt her—"

The spirit inched closer, forming a smirk as it watched them. "Alex would never hurt the door of light. She's quite safe. Funny, my father would've been over the moon to have her train here in his lifetime, and my brother is ecstatic as well, but not for the same reason. My father would have wanted to understand and explore her power. I can only imagine the things she'll accomplish when Alex succeeds." She laughed. "*If* he succeeds—but my brother is a bore, only wants his wife and child back from the dead."

What the hell?

The door of light: a door between life and death.

Gasping, Emmie glanced over her shoulder. Jason was standing inches behind her, still holding her arm as if to pull her out of the way at a moment's notice. His eyes were wide and his face was pale. The stark realization had hit him too. Temper House was way crazier than they had imagined, and Sarah was in big danger.

Another fact struck her: running would do no good. This woman had killed Dr. Albright and Howard, and she intended to kill them in the same way. They had walked right into her hands, and she was playing with them. A deep sense of dread swept through Emmie, but she still maneuvered backward, her heart racing.

The spirit inched closer. "Are you still planning to rescue her? Don't you understand yet?"

A wave of warmth radiated through Emmie on a deep, psychical level that she'd never felt before. A flash of light flared from the spirit's eyes like a surge of plasma and stretched out toward her chest. The skin beneath Emmie's shirt burned as if a red-hot poker had pressed against her.

Emmie lurched back and screamed, covering the area with her hand.

Jason rushed forward and stood between them, facing the spirit as if he might do better than she. "You'll stay away from us."

His sudden confrontation interrupted the spirit's attack on Emmie. It paused with a stunned expression, then tilted its head. "What an odd thing to say. I take it you're suggesting your psychic power can somehow influence me?" She gave a deep, loud laugh. "I have the upper hand here, my friend—dozens of upper hands if you include Dr. Albright's and Howard's—but I pity you. I really do. Your gift isn't worth my time."

A flash of light crossed the air and Jason cried out in pain as he stumbled back before falling. He groaned and winced as he lay on his side, clutching his chest as if someone had struck him.

The spirit turned its attention back to Emmie. "But you... *you* caught my eye just as Sarah did to my brother. It astonishes me that Dr. Albright could have missed such a powerful gift as yours. If he had only seen what I see now... He always wasted too much time trying to keep people like me from discovering the true nature of the psychic world. But what I've accomplished in the last year is light years ahead of anything Dr. Albright and his minions did in decades. I'm everything they wished they could be."

"You murdered them," Emmie said.

The spirit seemed to smile coyly. "I assimilated the best."

Emmie tensed and prepared to help Jason up and make a run for the back door. Before she could break away from the spirit, however, the woman's flaring light suddenly dimmed. The woman screamed as if someone had stabbed her in the heart, and she hunched forward with her light scattering in every direction. The intense light flashed and flickered, and within the chaos, the woman screamed, "Alex! Oh, my brother! What have you done?"

Struggling to make sense of the moment, Emmie understood that she was witnessing the woman's true, unshielded spirit for the first time. Its intensity had dropped to a glowing haze, as if the sun had suddenly switched off.

With her gaze still locked on the hobbled spirit, Emmie expected it might rise again to strike her down at any moment, but it had turned away, its face full of pain. Turning back for a moment to Emmie, the spirit glared with sharp predator eyes. But there was a deep sadness within the fury.

It would kill me now if it could.

Emmie stepped back and began calling Sarah's name over and over. Jason struggled to his feet and called with her, but their voices died in the silence.

The spirit faded as they yelled, drawn back within the cord of light, but before it left their presence, Emmie sensed a chance to reach in and restrain it. A moment of clarity and weakness when she could stop it in its tracks and hold it captive.

But what then? Fear swept through her, and the moment passed.

The spirit surged away in a streak of light, and it was gone.

Jason tugged at her arm, holding his side. "Em, run."

She spun around and ran.

✺ 33 ✺

E mmie and Jason rushed out the back door of the house, still calling out Sarah's name. The trees and plants rustled in a cool breeze as they headed straight toward the garden. No sign of their friends, but she spotted a piercing white light off in the distance between the trees.

Emmie gestured toward it. "That's got to be Sarah."

"Why not the madwoman?"

"Different light."

"You're right, because I can't see it."

"It's coming from the zoo," Emmie said. "That can't be good."

The sun had gone down behind a wall of dark clouds, and beyond the backyard a scattered array of solar lights had come to life, showing the winding path through the garden.

Trees swayed in the cool December breeze that brushed through Emmie's hair as they hurried toward the garden lights. But a flurry of activity in the tree branches above them caught her attention. Like a flock of birds stirring in the canopies, it seemed to follow them as they moved along, keeping pace even as they hurried.

"Something's following us."

Jason followed her gaze. "I heard it too."

Emmie rushed ahead, but paused at the edge of the zoo to catch her breath and stare up into the branches again. Whatever was moving in the trees stopped at the same time.

"It's watching us," she said.

"Lorelei?"

"We would see her light. An animal?"

The leaves rustled as soon as she started moving again. Jason circled around and viewed the tree from beneath the lower branches that swayed the most, taking out his phone and using the screen in flashlight mode. "I don't see anything."

Emmie turned toward the light coming from the large domed building in the center of the zoo. The light was brighter now, and some of the animals were screeching and causing a commotion.

Despite the disturbance, nobody outside the property would hear them. The satellite maps had showed the thick swamp encircling the zoo. A perfect natural barrier to prevent the animals from escaping, and no neighbors to disturb.

And nobody to hear their cries for help.

The light from the building was stronger now, and there was no mistaking its distinct characteristics. Sarah was there.

They ran faster toward the building. Several branches snapped and leaves dropped around her, but she didn't bother to glance around anymore. Whatever it was, she could only hope it wouldn't get in their way.

But after they crossed the threshold into the zoo, a branch cracked directly overhead and a screech filled the air as a massive creature swung down and landed on its feet in front of her.

Emmie screamed and stumbled back into Jason. It stood like a human, but a foot shorter than she was, with a thin, mangy layer of fur over its body. It let out a long, raspy cry that chilled her spine. Its lifeless eyes were sunken beneath furrowed brows, and it stood with its chin up, chest out and arms at its sides as if ready to attack.

In the faint light, she recognized that it was some sort of monkey. An orangutan? But nothing about it was... right. The thing was all wrong, quite unlike the ones she had seen in the zoo. The animal's flesh was dry and gray, with deep cracks at its joints, and its sparse fur was muddy and matted against its skin. Its snarling face was barely visible, but it stared at Emmie intently as if to make it clear that she would not be going further. Its movements were slow and wide, but she sensed its power even as it wobbled on its feet as if drunk. As it stepped toward her, she spotted an open wound on its chest that should have made it bleed to death, judging by the depth of it. Its rib cage showed two broken bones, and some of the internal organs were missing.

The thing should be dead.

It lurched cautiously toward them a few inches.

Emmie jumped back, with Jason nudging her toward a small structure to their left. It was a domed stone structure with two large pillars on either side. A metal door in the front was wide open, but everything inside was darkness. The building looked not much different than the other structures around them; no doubt another animal cage.

"Go there." Jason still pushed her toward it.

"We'll be trapped."

"Not inside. There's a shovel."

She spotted the flat head shovel by the open door. They moved slowly toward it at first, circling around the orangutan as it watched them, but as they approached the door, Emmie scrambled ahead and grabbed the shovel while raising it defensively against the animal.

The orangutan had not followed them. Instead, it stood defiantly taller, almost still, and stared into the doorway as if transfixed by their escape.

"What is it doing?" Emmie asked. "Why doesn't he follow us?"

Jason stared into the darkened doorway. "It knows what's in there, maybe?"

Emmie glanced back into the darkness as Jason held out his phone in flashlight mode to light the way. The cage inside was littered with stripped logs on a dirt floor and dozens of stones and small boulders lined the perimeter. Judging by the layout of the bare branches, small tracks and the maze-like habitat inside the cage, the animal must have been the size of a football. Two metal dishes sat just outside a rock formation at the back that looked like a cave. A wire fence running up to the ceiling would have separated them from whatever lurked beyond it, but the fence was mangled and pulled up in one corner.

"It's empty," she said.

Something metallic banged and echoed within the darkness. A metal bucket in the corner had toppled over, and an animal's black eyes glowed in the reflected light of the phone. Its body was obscured behind a pile of dirty rags.

"A raccoon?" Emmie asked.

"Let's freaking hope so."

She turned back to the orangutan. The thing had moved in closer while staring at them with its mouth wide open, revealing rotting teeth and a lifeless tongue. The dry, raspy air moved in and out of its lungs until the ape sounded like someone struggling to stay alive on a respirator.

While facing the orangutan directly, Emmie backed into the doorway and lowered the shovel. She looked at Jason. "Got any ideas?"

Jason looked around the cage, then hurried over to another door to their left and opened it. After examining the lock, he turned back to her. "The locks are sliding bolts. We can trap him in here."

"What if he doesn't come in?" Emmie asked.

"He will."

Emmie eyed him. "I hope you're not going to try *persuading* that thing. He won't respond to you."

Jason smirked. "You don't give me enough credit. Wasn't thinking of it *that* way. Just plain bait and switch."

"I don't like the sound of that."

Behind her, he closed the door partway, both hands clutching the edge as he peered back at the orangutan. The door creaked as he shifted it. "I'll stand near the back door with you. After he comes inside, I'll distract him while you run around the outside and lock the other door."

She let out a skeptical, "Yeah."

"Got a better idea?"

Her mind drew a blank. Running didn't seem like an option, as the thing would only chase them, and they couldn't reach Sarah with an animal like that, some sort of zombie, stalking them. "No."

Jason glanced around, then stepped into the doorway. Extending his hand toward the orangutan, he pretended to offer it food and spoke in a sweet tone, "Come inside. We have some delicious food for you."

The thing didn't move, but its unblinking eyes never looked away. It didn't need to eat, anyway.

Jason made wider gestures and rubbed his fingers together. The animal bared its teeth again with a guttural grunt.

"This isn't going to work." Still, Emmie moved to the back door, opened it and prepared to do her part.

"Sure it will." Jason extended his hands further and beckoned to it. "Come here, big guy."

The animal narrowed its eyes and inched ahead.

Pushing back a wave of panic, Emmie held the door open with one hand, the shovel in the other.

The orangutan walked forward cautiously as Jason continued to coax it toward the door. The phone still lit the ground, moving with each step he took backwards. After the orangutan stood in the doorway, it stopped and suddenly turned to Emmie as if she had somehow startled it.

Jason snapped his fingers. "Look at me. Look at me."

The nightmarish decay over the animal's body became clear as it stood before them. It huffed at Emmie a few more times, but then turned its attention back to Jason as he led the thing further inside. Jason had almost made it to the back door, but then the ape stopped.

Still gripping the metal door handle, Emmie prepared to run around to the front. Jason wouldn't be far behind her.

But something in the room let out a piercing shriek. The animal that had crouched in the shadows now emerged and charged toward her. Its wide jaws snapped at her ankles as she jumped back. She had seen those bat-like ears, sharp fangs, over-sized whiskers and black fur in zoos before.

A Tasmanian devil.

With rotting flesh like the orangutan's, the devil whipped at her ankles, its leathery snout brushing against her skin as clumps of dried flesh dangled from the edges of its mouth.

Emmie swung the shovel toward it, knocking the animal to the side as she scrambled to get outside.

Jason wasn't far behind. Together, they managed to get the door shut, but Jason struggled with the bolt on the lock. "It's rusted."

He glanced over at Emmie, meeting her gaze as his expression relaxed a little. "Run, Em. You find Sarah. Got it?"

Before Emmie could answer, the orangutan crashed through the door.

Jason stood between them defiantly and met her gaze. "Run!"

She hesitated. How could she abandon him?

But Jason turned away from her and drew the animal's attention, prodding it and yelling out commands as if he still had a chance to control it psychically. The orangutan lunged toward him, its huffing breaths growing louder and louder, and Emmie was about to take another swing at it with the shovel when Jason ran off, still luring it with himself as the bait. Emmie's heart sank when the ape followed him.

They charged deeper into the zoo, the animal surging after

Jason at a steady pace, although its erratic gait slowed it. Jason was agile, sprinting around the edge of another domed structure and stumbling through a patch of brush along the way.

She caught a final glimpse of him in the faint light, his eyes wide, before he disappeared into the darkness. The animal's shrieks rose above Jason's heaving gasps for breath, but within seconds the cries from the other startled animals in the cages nearby drowned them out, and they were gone.

❧ 34 ❧

Emmie couldn't find them. She raced forward in the direction where Jason and the orangutan had disappeared while screaming Jason's name. Some of the animals in the nearby cages howled and screeched back at her, masking any chance of hearing their footsteps, but she followed them as far as she could, winding around the cages until she encountered the metal fence that lined the property and the swampy darkness beyond that. Only after sensing her vulnerability did she stop.

She had lost him. The panic swelled in her mind, and she needed to do something.

Get Sarah out.

Jason had risked his life to lead the orangutan away from her for just that reason. She could only hope that he'd get away; she had to take advantage of the opportunity he'd given her. Turning back toward the center of the zoo, where she had seen Sarah's light earlier, she followed her instincts—or was it still panic?—to find her friend.

Still gripping the shovel in one hand, she stepped lightly, peering around the corners of the structures and expecting that anything might be waiting for her on the other side. Each time she was met with more darkness, the cries of agitated animals and the pervasive smell of their food, excrement and body odor. Sometimes she spotted their eyes watching her from their cages, reflecting the faint light from the solar lamps. She was never alone.

Arriving at a large cage, she spotted the occupant staring back at her, and her blood ran cold. An orangutan. She gasped and stumbled backwards, but it wasn't the same one that had chased after Jason—its features were a little different: slightly darker fur, a more rounded face, and an obvious limp as it inched back when she approached. This one sat in the corner peacefully staring back at her with tired eyes. This one was alive, although alone.

Her gaze skimmed over the plaque outside the door of the cage. Sumatran Orangutan. It listed two names, Shiva and Parvati, although someone had attempted to cross out Shiva's name with black paint.

Emmie stared at the creature and spoke softly, "What did they do to you? The other one is your mate, isn't it? And somehow it got out."

The orangutan remained expressionless, although tilted its head a bit.

But the reality of her situation crashed in again. There wasn't time to contemplate an animal's trauma, and she continued on her way. The spiral top of the structure where Sarah's light had shined so brightly earlier towered over the other cages. It was just around the corner.

She hurried ahead, determined to plow through any obstacle to get to her friend, and spotted the building's door. No sign of anyone nearby. The light of something flickering inside came through the narrow opaque windows on either side of the door. A faint, familiar smell drifted under her nose. Something was burning.

Emmie hurried to reach the door.

A white light flashed in front of her. She stopped and shielded her eyes as it expanded rapidly into the angel of death.

Lorelei's spirit lit the area, blocking her path to the door. Emmie clenched the shovel in her hands, even knowing it was useless in the moment. She wouldn't run this time.

"Admiring our pets?" Lorelei's spirit asked.

Emmie straightened, ready to face whatever the woman threw at her. "You experimented on them."

"I did no such thing. You have my brother to blame for the abominations running loose on our property, but I don't mind so much. They're perfect guard dogs, in a sense, alerting me to anyone who trespasses."

Emmie glanced over her shoulder.

"Do you really think you can run?" Lorelei inched closer. "You are stronger than Dr. Albright, physically, but he was an old man, and I burned through him like paper. I would've thought his psychic defenses stronger, considering he was a master at Carey Kali. But that's what happens when people get all holier-than-thou about developing their gifts." She laughed. "How are they going to stop spirits that don't have those inhibitions? I sure don't have any."

"What do you want?" Emmie demanded.

"You." Lorelei stared at her intensely.

Emmie glanced beyond Lorelei's spirit at the door to the building and yelled, "Sarah!"

"You're just going to attract Shiva's attention. Is that what you want? He has a tendency to react abruptly and violently to strangers, especially at night. Another of my brother's failures, but he was so hopelessly reckless after all. But I won't prolong your fear like I did with Dr. Albright. He deserved all the pain and suffering, don't you think?"

The image of Howard's burned body flashed through her mind. "Nobody deserves to die like Howard and Albright."

"Albright killed my father!" Lorelei's spirit screamed, spewing shards of light. "He killed my mother! That Howard started it all, telling Albright my parents were doing forbidden things after my father asked him for information *as a friend*. Betrayed by that snitch! They left three orphans, and why? Because we wouldn't obey him. We wouldn't do what they said. Just a small group of psychics carrying on with our lives and honing our skills. We weren't going out to hurt anyone, but still Albright and the others came *to give orders.*"

"You don't even see it, do you?" Emmie replied, though she knew it wasn't wise. "The zombie animals here, you burning people to death, your brother trying to bring back his family from the other side. You've all been going mad in this house for a long time, and Albright knew it would happen. He may have been arrogant, but he was right."

Lorelei scoffed. "Oh, well. You can discuss it with him on the other side, and all the others who died unnaturally while my spirit grew into the stuff of legends." Lorelei moved forward and spoke tenderly now, ignoring everything Emmie had said. "Your spirit, though, is safe with me. And it won't be so difficult to take it from you, even if you resist. Believe me, I'm not completely evil. You haven't done anything to me, and so I wish there was some way I could retrieve your gift without stripping away your soul, but that's the way this works."

A flash of light flared from Lorelei's eyes and reached out like a tendril toward Emmie. She focused on the spirit, holding it in her mind like she had done to so many other spirits, but Sarah had always been there to release them, to disarm them. Sarah wasn't there now to complete the act. Emmie could restrain Lorelei, but something in her body and mind burned as if someone had focused the sun's rays on her through a magnifying glass.

This is what Dr. Albright and Howard went through before they died. She strained to escape the intense heat, but her muscles were paralyzed within the light. She opened her mouth to scream again. Nothing came out.

The energy shuddered through her like a million volts of electricity, and Emmie's spirit slipped out of her body toward Lorelei's light. Searing pain stabbed at her every cell.

Suddenly, the pain stopped.

Something flashed brighter around them, encompassing not only her, but Lorelei. Emmie's spirit snapped back into her body as if someone had dropped her from a pool of molten lava into a lake of ice. She convulsed when she hit the ground, the shovel clattering to a stop beside her, and caught her breath. Sarah's voice shouted from somewhere nearby, "Leave her alone!"

35

Sarah squeezed Finn against her. His skin was cold as if he'd just stepped out of a refrigerator, but there wasn't time to warm him up. They embraced for only a few seconds before hurrying out of the pavilion, leaving a pile of corpses behind.

As soon as they were outside, a familiar face stared up at them from the ground. Emmie. She was lying on her side with a blinding white spirit hovering over her. The spirit's face was unmistakable: Lorelei's. But the aura radiating from the being was unlike anything Sarah had seen before. No gentle blues and golds like a dying patient's. This woman's colors struck her with harsh reds and grays. Colors of a twisted soul. Colors of death.

A white extension of Lorelei's spirit reached toward Emmie even as she lay helpless on the ground.

Sarah scrambled toward her friend as rage swelled in her chest. The warm light she had used so many times to gently nudge patients to move on now surged, and she directed it like a sword toward the heart of Lorelei's spirit. She didn't hold back. Every bit of her energy focused on stopping the woman. "Leave her alone!"

Lorelei's spirit ignited in a white-hot blaze as Sarah's light hit her in the chest. The woman's spirit shuddered, but she stopped her attack on Emmie, pulling back and glancing around with an expression of annoyed confusion before finally meeting Sarah's gaze. There was a sparkle of pleasure in the spirit's eyes as if their confrontation was a game. And before Sarah could push her again, Lorelei's spirit swept away into thin air like a flash of lightning.

With a racing heart, Sarah rushed to Emmie's side and checked her wounds. The spirit had burned a hole through Emmie's shirt and then her flesh, and her skin was already blistering from the blazing energy. "It could have been worse."

Emmie winced while touching her chest just below the wound. "It feels worse."

Sarah propped her up, but Emmie continued struggling to get to her feet and finally stood on her own. They exchanged embraces.

"You need to get to a doctor," Sarah said.

Scoffing, Emmie plucked a shovel off the ground. She tapped it against her palm and jabbed the end into the air like a sword toward an invisible foe. "I can deal with her."

"No, you can't." Finn joined them. "Listen to me, that woman has some serious power. You said so yourself."

"Didn't you feel it?" Sarah asked.

Emmie glanced down. "I felt it all right." She looked at Finn. "You can see it too?" When he nodded, she added, "So can Jason. I'm guessing it's because she isn't dead?"

"Who the hell knows?" Finn said. "Let's figure it out later and get out now?"

Sarah held Emmie's hand. "Yes, we should leave now, before she comes back. We can get help from other psychics."

"What other psychics?" Emmie asked. "She killed Dr. Albright and Jason's friend Howard, and maybe more. How is anyone going to stop her?"

"Hey, guys, where *is* Jason?" Finn asked.

They looked around. Emmie pointed into the darkness beyond the zoo. "It chased him!"

"What did?"

"An orangutan. Like, a dead one."

"Oh, no..." Sarah groaned. "It seems like there's a bunch of these things."

Finn stepped toward the darkness. "We can't leave Jason out there."

"I'll find him," Emmie said. "Stay with Sarah. Go back to the car, and we'll catch up with you. But lie low until we get there. We should all be together if we face Lorelei again."

Sarah looked at her friend. "If she comes back..."

"I won't be a hero. I'll run. I promise. But if I don't return in an hour, just get to safety without me, understand? I'll get Jason out through the swamp if I have to."

Sarah and Finn headed back toward the car as Emmie moved off into the darkness, using her phone to light the way.

Only minutes after they had separated, another light caught Sarah's attention. A point of brightness, hovering in their path straight ahead. It beamed at them for several seconds before rapidly expanding into a fiery spirit form. They had made it to the edge of the zoo when she appeared, just before reaching the garden. Sarah could hear the animals stirring again within their cages. The branches above them swayed.

Finn pulled himself up when the woman appeared, but Sarah moved forward. The spirit watched them now with amusement.

"Lorelei. I can deal with her," Sarah said.

"Your bravery is endearing," Lorelei said.

Sarah grabbed Finn's wrist firmly. "Go to the meeting point. Please. Don't follow me, or I might not be able to do it."

"All right," he whispered, meeting her gaze.

After he hesitated, she squeezed his wrist. "Trust me."

Finn nodded once and hurried away.

Sarah turned toward the spirit and focused. It was just a spirit after all, no different from the ones she had released so many times before with Emmie's help. This one might resist, but she sensed her fear and pain.

She held Lorelei's spirit in her mind, feeling the stubborn resistance to her intrusion, but Sarah filled it with the same warmth and peace that she had given to many dying patients. The spirit reacted to her confrontation by backing into the darkness, away from the zoo. Sarah stepped toward it, repelling its growing defiance while also pushing it toward the afterlife.

"If you kill me," Lorelei said quietly. "You'll be no better than me. The spirit doesn't move on so easily when it still clings to the body. You haven't quite mastered your gift yet, I can see. No chance that you'll beat me. You can only become me."

"Lies." With Lorelei on the defensive, Sarah pushed her back further away from Emmie and Finn. She just needed to give her friends enough time to get out of there. And if Jason was in trouble, she wouldn't stop until she found him too.

But a nagging voice interrupted her concentration. *She* had caused this mess.

Lorelei seemed to seize on the moment and thrust back toward her. "This is for my brother."

The spirit's blinding white light intensified and eclipsed Sarah's own. An energy surge startled her, and it took every ounce of strength to keep Lorelei's raging spirit from reaching her friends.

The confrontation had worked the animals into a frenzy inside their cages. They banged against the bars, shrieked and cried, and Sarah felt all their fear and confusion.

Despite the overwhelming push forward, Lorelei circled around her, and moved further into the darkness of the zoo, all the time prodding and poking at Sarah's defenses.

"It's just a matter of time," Lorelei said. "You don't have the stamina."

"Alex set himself up—"

"To fail! Yes, I know. His modus operandi." Lorelei laughed. "It's not about him. None of this is about him. You still don't understand, do you? So naïve. Your gift is all I want. To round out my collection."

Sarah stared back. "You can't be the door of light. It doesn't work that way, and you know it."

"No, I can't. And no one should be that. I'll save everyone a lot of bother and just take your light. Why do I need to heal anyone anyway?"

Lorelei continued backing away as Sarah advanced on her, circling around cage after cage and moving off the main path into a section of the zoo that she hadn't visited before. The trees were thick around them, and the light colliding between both sizzled and lit up the area like a blown transformer.

As she moved out further into the depths of a darkened zoo, a rustling swept through the branches around her. A moment later, something heavy and alive thumped on the ground behind her. She spun around as an impoverished animal grabbed her with cold, coarse hands. It was only slightly shorter than her, and it looked at her with empty, dead eyes. Pulling her closer, the thing screeched and howled as if it had won a great victory. Sarah wrestled away its icy, leathery hands, but its long boney arms stretched out around her chest and squeezed. Her breath escaped suddenly, and she struggled to inhale.

An orangutan. A physical creature she couldn't fight.

As soon as it embraced her, something jumped on its back. Finn had disregarded her and followed them, and now he jumped at the beast as soon as it touched her. He pounded the orangutan in the head and neck, while letting out a string of curses that filled the night air. Whatever strength he'd lost in the mausoleum had flooded back in a torrent as he came alive with rage. After tearing away a chunk of flesh from the orangutan's shoulder, he stared at it in shock before dropping it. But his actions only seemed to further incite the animal's violence.

Finding a breath, Sarah gasped.

Lorelei's energy flared forward and struck Sarah in the chest, even striking the animal in the process. The three of them flew backwards and the animal released its grip on her. Within the burning light, she got her first clear view of the orangutan. It had the same undead flesh as the bobcat in the garden.

Finn had done a mad thing to save her, and he had fallen and rolled into the brush, but he was moving.

Without another thought, Sarah focused sharply on the animal's spirit. She pushed it out, but the animal resisted. Sarah pushed it harder, and a moment later a burning flash erupted within the ape's body. A white flame consumed its flesh, burning it from the inside out as its spirit hovered above them. Its body collapsed and burned from its chest outward until the flames died out, leaving only its head and lower legs intact.

Finn had returned and now stood over it with clenched fists, as if ready to beat it down again if it rose.

Lorelei had watched and said nothing all this while, but now she spoke. "Now you are like me. Now you understand."

Sarah prepared to send the animal's spirit away. "I put it out of its misery."

"Exactly! It's an act of love, you see. Love is kind."

"You have no idea what love is."

"And you do?"

"I'll never be like you."

"Too late."

Sarah released the animal's spirit and its light flashed away into the night sky.

Lorelei didn't wait to strike again. She caught Sarah a moment before she could defend herself. The pain and heat struck her in the chest and filled Sarah's body, as if someone had thrown her into an oven.

Nursing burns on her chest and arms, Sarah also began pushing at Lorelei's spirit with more strength than she thought possible. The woman cried out. It was working.

"Just... like... me," Lorelei said between pained gasps.

The truth of Lorelei's words struck Sarah. For a moment, it disarmed her as the thought came, *Am I really like her?*

A wave of darkness swept through her mind. She would be

killing a woman whose body was somewhere else, still alive, strong and healthy.

As if she'd read Sarah's mind, Lorelei grinned and said, "Now you get it. You'd be killing me, Sarah. Not releasing my spirit in your goody-goody way but killing a person. Because you are right, it's the only way to stop me!"

She's messing with my mind. There had to be a way to imprison the woman's spirit without killing her body, and Sarah had to find it, or her friends wouldn't get out alive.

The darkness lifted from her mind as her strength returned. She pushed at Lorelei's spirit to the edge of ripping it away from her body. But despite her resolve to stop the woman at any cost, she couldn't complete the act.

Lorelei's words hung in her mind. *You're just like me.*

"No, I'm not." Sarah held the woman's spirit within her mind, but Lorelei's resistance to letting go prevented her from ending the struggle.

Lorelei stared back at her with a grin.

36

Emmie raced along through the darkness at the edge of the zoo, calling out Jason's name with the shovel in one hand and her phone in flashlight mode in the other. The trees rustled around her, and her ears perked at the faintest noises. How far could he have gone? Shouting into the darkness was far from ideal—any wild animals certainly knew she was there—but she was running out of time. Twice, she cautiously veered in a new direction after her phone's light reflected off a pair of glowing eyes hidden within the weeds and brush.

Lights flashed behind her, and her heart sank. Had Lorelei returned? She tensed with the anxious dread of confronting the woman again, even as she called Jason's name more loudly.

Seconds later, something cracked in the trees nearby. She stopped walking, lifted her shovel and her ears perked up. The steady rhythm of her feet scraping against the ground had stopped, and she held her breath while the leaves rustled around her.

A figure appeared only a few yards behind them.

Then a familiar, weak voice spoke from the darkness as the figure stepped out of the shadows. "Emmie. Oh, thank God."

It was Jason, walking toward her with hunched shoulders

and a look of distress and relief. There were dried bloodstains on his face and shirt as if he'd been in a violent fight. The sleeve of his shirt was torn, his pants were muddy, and his hair stuck out in all directions. He opened his arms when he got close.

Emmie did the same. "Jason!"

"Finally," he said.

She embraced him. "What happened?"

Jason attempted to straighten his hair. "What *didn't* happen to me? I got turned around while trying to stay away from that thing attacking me."

Another flash of light behind them caught their attention. Jason gestured toward it. "Is that Sarah?"

"And Lorelei. I found them, but I came to find you."

"You almost found me dead. That freaking thing kicked my ass. Then, for some reason, it just left."

"Maybe it thought you *were* dead. Lucky you got away." She examined the blood. "Can you walk?"

"Yes."

She glanced back toward the surging light. "We have to get back to them and stop Lorelei. I'm not sure how long Sarah can hold her off alone."

"Agreed."

They hurried toward the light, but another disturbance within the darkness caught their attention. Shuffling footsteps and gasping breaths. Emmie focused the light on the source of the noises. She tensed and listened, expecting that the orangutan had caught up and would jump out at them at any second, but instead a young woman's figure appeared standing in the shadows, her face turned down as she shielded her eyes from Emmie's light.

"No, no, no," the woman said.

It was the same woman who had struggled to descend the stairs in the house earlier. She stood propped up beside a tree with a cane in one hand to steady herself.

The woman giggled like a girl and spoke in a melodic rhyme, "Little Bo Peep, lost her sheep."

Emmie approached her cautiously. "You're Cecilia. Is that right?"

Cecilia stopped talking and stared at them without moving.

"Your sister is trying to kill us."

"Love is patient," Cecilia said.

"I wouldn't exactly call what she's doing an act of love." Emmie stepped toward her and gestured toward the flashing lights across the zoo. "Can you please help us? We need to save our friends."

Cecilia nodded.

"Okay, good. How can we stop her?"

The woman gestured back toward the house. "The body is the temple."

"I don't understand." Emmie looked in the direction she had indicated. The poor woman was mad, and yet she was their only hope. "How can we stop your sister? What do we need to do?"

Jason touched Emmie's shoulder. "Wait a minute." He turned to Cecilia. "Your sister's alone in the house now?"

Cecilia nodded again.

"I see," Emmie said. "We can get to her while she's projecting. I'm guessing she can't fight in two places at once." She turned back to Cecilia. "Can you lead us to her?"

Another nod. The woman struggled to stand and wobbled for a few steps, but then kept pace with them using her cane as they headed toward the house. Her wide eyes often glanced over her shoulder along the way, as if something might attack them at any moment, but within minutes they'd arrived at the house's back porch.

The windows of the house showed the reflection of flashes going off behind them as if they were fireworks. Looking back, Emmie spotted the source in the distance. The colors and intensity were unmistakable, like someone's signature. Sarah's light.

"Something wrong?" Jason asked.

"Sarah's in trouble. We have to act fast." Emmie headed toward the back door, but Cecilia extended her arm and stopped them. "What's wrong?"

Cecilia gestured toward the upper floor of the house.

"Lorelei is upstairs?" Jason asked.

"Love is patient. Love is kind," Cecilia said.

"I'll take that as a yes," Jason said. "Please take us to her."

All the windows along the second floor of the house were dark, except for one at the far corner.

Cecilia turned away and walked to the back door. She opened it and held it for them while looking down as if she had done something wrong. Emmie tossed the shovel into the grass. The dangers they faced now wouldn't be beaten with such a simple weapon.

Feeling more vulnerable than ever, she struggled forward up the steps and inside with Jason right behind her. Cecilia put her index finger against her puckered lips. "Shhh..."

They paused as Cecilia shuffled along ahead of them, limping and dragging herself along with only half of her body seeming to cooperate. She used a railing along the side of the hallway to prop herself up as she led them through the house to the main stairway near the entrance.

As they stood at the bottom of the stairs, Cecilia pointed to the right wing of the house.

Emmie nodded once.

"This might be a trap," Jason whispered.

Emmie thought for a moment, then shook her head. "We're out of time anyway."

Paying no attention to their brief conversation, Cecilia continued up the stairs without stopping while dragging herself along with great difficulty. Jason stealthily moved up beside Cecilia and grabbed hold of the woman's arm. She stopped for a moment as if considering his intentions, staring into his eyes like a frightened animal, and then she accepted his help, clutching at him with a bashful grin.

Their footsteps faintly echoed through the house as Cecilia led them down the hallway toward the left wing of the house.

The lights at the far end of the hallway were either burned out or switched off. Emmie didn't bother to ask but instead trusted this woman's guidance. As they approached a set of large double doors at the end of the hallway, Jason glanced over at her suddenly, his eyes wide and his face full of concern.

I feel it too. There were spirits ahead. She could feel their energy strongly now, more than any spirit she'd ever felt, and they were behind those doors.

Cecilia paused at the entrance. Her tight lips and strained expression seemed to warn them of the dangers inside. She pulled a key out of her pocket and used it to open the door, twisting it in the lock with great care. The right door opened inward, squeaking on its rusty hinges, and Cecilia gestured for them to go inside.

Emmie spotted the glow as soon as the door opened. It was streaming out from under a closed door straight ahead. A familiar light. The same psychic energy that had emanated from Lorelei's spirit during her encounter with Howard. The woman *was* in there.

They stepped into the short hallway together, with Cecilia cowering beside the double doors with her hands clasped together. Emmie rubbed her arms. The air was cool in that space, as if someone had left a window open, although there were no windows in sight.

Passing several open doorways, they arrived at the last door and went inside without waiting for Cecilia's help. They moved cautiously. Emmie shivered; the temperature couldn't have been more than forty degrees in there, like in a butcher's freezer. Across the room she spotted the source of the chill. A massive air conditioner filled an entire window and whirred hypnotically.

The light was coming from somewhere just around the corner ahead. Navigating around some bedroom furniture and clutter, Emmie led them forward without stopping, although

Jason clutched the back of her arm. She pulled him closer as she came around the corner of a wall and stepped into the glow.

A shifting sphere of energy pulsed at the far side of the room. The sphere's shell was alive with dozens of spirits swarming around a center figure sitting on the floor at its core.

Lorelei.

❧ 37 ❧

Lorelei sat naked and motionless within the sphere of spirits, her body obscured within the swirling ghostly haze, and faced a single white rose on a small table a few feet in front of her.

She made no reaction as Emmie and Jason stepped into the room to get a better view of her, but the woman's bare back revealed large patches of reddened skin like sunburns, some more severe than others. Despite the chilly air, a great heat emanated from the sphere and grew stronger as they approached her. It was like standing in front of an open oven.

The dozens of spirits circling Lorelei stared with cold and expressionless eyes into the room's drab darkness, peering around without blinking as if guarding the woman. Emmie recognized two of the spirits immediately: Dr. Albright and Howard. Their faces swept by several times within a minute, and her courage faltered at seeing her former mentor trapped in Lorelei's power. All the spirits looped endlessly around the woman, each caught in a different orbit.

Emmie approached the woman cautiously with Jason at her side, expecting that she might turn around and attack them at any moment. A strange energy filled the air. Emmie stretched out her hand, allowing the energy to pulse and tingle through her fingertips as if she were getting too close to some sort of Tesla coil.

The swirling apparitions noticed them, meeting Emmie's gaze for only a moment each time they circled the sphere. If Lorelei was aware of the intrusion behind her, she wasn't doing anything about it. Not yet anyway.

Dr. Albright's spirit hovered briefly closer during one of the passes, and Emmie focused on him, pulling him toward her.

She had received telepathic messages from him as a child in his office, but now she heard nothing. Still, that didn't stop her from trying to reach him.

Do you see me?

His eyes flickered like candles as a moment of recognition swept through him, but as quickly as it had formed, it disappeared.

He's still in there.

She tried again, *Come away from her.*

A connection surged between them like the silence on an open phone line, with the anticipation for the caller to speak. Something was holding him back. She sensed the paralysis in his thoughts.

I'll get you out of there... somehow.

A thin, almost imperceptible cord trailed behind Dr. Albright's spirit, the same connection that she'd earlier seen trailing from Lorelei's spirit downstairs. She had almost missed it. The other spirits were connected in the same way, with each tether leading back to Lorelei's forehead, although she was still turned away from them. No doubt it prevented the spirits from escaping and somehow controlled their actions.

Emmie studied the cord and their movements as they endlessly swirled around Lorelei, the energy flaring off the spirits and drawing back into her body, leaving a minor burn on her skin as it entered.

She's feeding off them. And that feeds the angel of death.

She glanced at Jason. Did he also see the spirits? She was afraid to ask for fear of breaking the silence, but he was also stretching his hand toward Lorelei, as if testing the waters. She watched his face change from curiosity to certainty, and he nodded. He saw them too.

While his hand was still extended, a spark of electricity bolted from one of the spirits and sparked against the end of Jason's outstretched fingertip. "Damn!"

They turned and stared at Lorelei with wide eyes.

Had she heard them?

Jason inched back defensively, although Lorelei hadn't reacted.

Emmie couldn't keep quiet any longer. "She's not here."

Her voice startled her as it filled the silence, but there was still no reaction from the woman or the spirits guarding her.

"If we can't get to her physically, how do we... shut her down?" Jason asked.

"Her consciousness is outside with her spirit. That makes sense. She's using the spirits here to act as her eyes and ears, but she can't be aware in two places at once."

"Maybe she can," Jason said.

"Let me try the others." Emmie focused on the sphere of spirits again.

Bringing the other spirits toward her also yielded no results. If only Sarah were there, maybe they could release the spirits together—but with Lorelei acting as an anchor, how far would they get? No chance Sarah could get them to pass on without somehow breaking the connection.

So how would they break the connection?

The spirits watched them. But why didn't they strike? Just a shock to Jason's finger?

That's it?

She wants us to catch us with our guard down. Lorelei isn't striking at us yet because she's focused on Sarah, but she'll return soon to finish us off. The woman was just in defensive mode now—in her *temple*—

while she struck at Sarah. Emmie couldn't help but feel a panic well up in her chest while thinking of her friend. Sarah was in danger. They needed to act *now*.

Emmie focused on Dr. Albright again, trying to communicate, pushing her thoughts toward him even if he couldn't return an answer.

How do we stop her?

She tried to force a response from him in her mind while opening her eyes and focusing on his spirit. Even just a gesture or a single word might reveal a clue. But his eyes met hers a few more times, staring back with only a dull recognition. Nothing came through on any level. *I forgive you, doctor. I know you would answer if you could.*

After a few more strained attempts with no luck, she resolved to turn to more drastic measures. She glanced around the room for a weapon they might use on Lorelei, but before she could locate anything, Jason had the same idea. He picked up an old desk chair and raised it over his head as if preparing to hurl it at the woman. Whatever it took to break her out of her attack on Sarah.

Before he could throw the chair, Cecilia stepped into the room. She slid herself along the wall as she inched closer and propped herself against one of the tables, but stayed by the door. She clutched her hands together, rubbing them nervously. "No, no, no."

Emmie jumped at Jason and gestured for him to stop. Though the chair was on the verge of flying, he restrained himself and lowered it to the floor.

"Then how do we stop her?" Emmie asked Cecilia.

Cecilia shook her head. "You can't. You can't."

"What will happen if we wake her up?" Jason asked.

"Ashes to ashes," Cecilia answered.

"There's got to be a way to stop her." Emmie rubbed her aching forehead. "Every moment we wait..."

"Love endures all things," Cecilia said.

❦ 38 ❧

F inn was afraid to touch Sarah. If only he could reach out and comfort her as she strained against Lorelei's spirit, but Sarah had said he might disrupt the energy that was holding the woman back.

Though he couldn't see ghosts, he could see Lorelei's light flaring from a formless figure, throwing off sparks and waves of heat as the two psychics clashed with blinding energy. The electric air pulsed through him and warmed his skin.

Sarah's face was full of pain, and Finn ached with a desperation to do something. He couldn't watch passively anymore, so he reached out and held her hand. Her skin was hot as if she were sick with a fever and her muscles were stiff, although she didn't seem to notice his touch. Her narrow gaze was fixed on Lorelei and her lips pressed together. The veins on her forehead bulged. He had never witnessed that level of focus in her eyes before, and her intensity scared him.

She had asked him not to interfere. He pulled his hand away and closed his eyes. As the heat swelled around them, he focused on the angelic vision of Sarah, letting it fill every dark corner in his mind. He wanted to reach out and embrace her, pull her to safety, but he couldn't help her. He wasn't psychic—not the slightest hint of psychic ability, as Natalia had put it—and his love for Sarah wouldn't help in a situation like this, would it?

Within the turmoil, he dared to break her concentration and whispered, "I love you."

If she'd heard him, she showed no reaction. But something had changed in the air, something between them. Her energy had faded for a moment, and a pang of guilt swept through him.

I weakened her, somehow.

Don't interfere.

A moment later, Sarah reached over without looking away and squeezed his hand. "I got this," she said.

Her warmth radiated through him as a powerful burst came from Lorelei's light.

He *was* breaking Sarah's focus, bringing her down.

Push that beautiful light of yours. Let's make things right.

She squeezed his hand more tightly, still without looking away from Lorelei. There was that same spark of light in her eyes that he had seen earlier as her warmth flared for a moment, sweeping through him and then fading away. Something had stirred in her, but she would need to magnify that by a thousand to end Lorelei's attack.

Sarah turned her face toward him for just a moment, and whispered, "I love you t—"

Suddenly she lurched back, stumbling to the ground as a violent, searing wind swept around them. The air seemed to burn Finn's lungs as he gasped for a breath while trying to shield Sarah from whatever had struck them.

But she was struggling to stand. He put his arm around her and lifted her to her feet. The moment of distraction had allowed Lorelei to catch her off guard. She balanced and focused again, raising her eyes to Lorelei, but she also wavered as sweat formed across her bare skin. Her hands trembled as she clenched her teeth and strained forward.

Fear rushed through Finn. *This is going to kill her.*

"I won't give up." She straightened for a moment and closed

her fists even as Lorelei's spirit continued the assault unabated. Sarah sank while trying to catch her breath.

What had Natalia said to him? His mind raced to remember something encouraging, *anything* that might help Sarah.

Fill your mind with light.

I did that, but Lorelei's not attacking me... not yet.

His frustration boiled over. He had to do something now or Sarah would die.

The growing realization that they might not make it out of there alive hit him with full force. The scorching heat was relentless and would consume them within minutes. Lorelei was just biding her time now, waiting for Sarah to wear herself out before moving in for the final kill.

Sarah's eyes still sparkled. *But that spark isn't enough. Someone's got to light that fire. Throw gasoline on it... or dynamite. Emotional dynamite.*

He stared into her drooping eyes.

It's time to light that spark.

Finn stepped in front of Lorelei's spirit so that he stood between them, then turned to face Sarah. Her eyes looked so beautiful in that moment as she looked at him. So tired. An excruciating heat blasted his skin as he moved backward into Lorelei's energy, all the time keeping his gaze on Sarah. He filled his mind again with the vision of Sarah as an angel. *His* angel.

Sarah's eyes widened in horror. Her despair only emboldened him to continue.

"Please, Finn, stay by me," she screamed. "Don't go near her."

Finn smelled burning flesh. *His* flesh and the pain threatened to break his concentration—but he didn't stop.

Dark magic cannot enter a mind full of light and joy.

Maybe it couldn't enter his mind, but he would have one hell of a sunburn at his funeral.

The intense heat soon grew unbearable. Sarah continued to scream for him to get out of there. He struggled to breathe and stumbled before collapsing to his knees without losing sight of her.

As the world swirled around him, with the pain pushing him to the edge of unconsciousness, he collapsed onto his side and turned his face toward Sarah.

Her expression had changed. She wasn't an angel anymore. She scowled as she pulled herself up with an alarming fearlessness.

The emotional dynamite had gone off. There was a deep rage in her eyes, and if he'd been able to see her light in that moment, he had no doubt it would have lit up the night sky. Her teeth bared, she glared at Lorelei's spirit with an intensity he had never seen in her before. Her fingers curled into claws, and she leaned forward as if she might lunge forward and strangle the woman, if Lorelei had stood there in physical form.

Lorelei's spirit flashed and blazed in a whirlwind of heat and intensity. The woman screamed and backed away as Sarah stepped forward with fuming determination. The animals in the zoo erupted in chaos, shrieking, howling and banging against the bars of the cages.

Sarah hovered at the edge of his view, and Finn lifted himself to watch her even as pain stabbed at every inch of his back. He wouldn't let her out of his sight.

His angel-turned-demon didn't relent. An energy ripped through the air. Lorelei's agonized voice cursed and screamed. Sarah didn't slow until the spirit had shattered into a million fiery fragments that exploded before them like a supernova. The dying sparks scattered in the air, the heat fading rapidly, before the pieces were swept away back toward the house.

❧ 39 ❧

Emmie considered Cecilia's cryptic words.

Ashes to ashes...

Love endures all things...

Bible references, but what was she expected to do with that?

No time to figure it out. She stepped toward Lorelei. Every second they waited gave the woman an opportunity to strike at Sarah. The spirits that circled Lorelei showed no emotion as they directed an incessant stare at the invaders. No doubt Lorelei had full control of their actions and would use their powers to defend her at any cost.

So what *was* their plan?

Disrupt her long enough to give Sarah the advantage.

But the ghostly haze of Lorelei's cocoon seemed to give them no way in. Emmie opened her eyes and met Jason's eyes. He solemnly looked back as if he also understood the futility in their efforts. This was over their heads. Not even Dr. Albright had survived the woman's attacks, so what chance did *she* have against her?

I can't let Sarah down.

She would focus on one of the spirits, peel them away one at a time to get to the core. She *had* nudged Dr. Albright after all.

Closing her eyes, Emmie strained with all her strength, focusing on Dr. Albright. The stress shook her body as she pulled on his spirit. Her pulse thumped in her ears. The energy of his spirit wavered and moved toward her, but it was like stretching a thick rubber band. No matter how hard she drew him in, the resistance grew.

I'm not strong enough.

She strained again, her body trembling this time. Whatever power Lorelei had over Dr. Albright was far beyond Emmie's ability. She sensed Dr. Albright's essence within her grasp, but something was magnifying the struggle. Some unseen force was dragging him down.

I can't...

She relaxed, releasing his spirit with a gasp.

Jason then embraced her, whispering in her ear, "We'll go in there together. On three?"

Emmie pulled back and nodded.

They turned and faced Lorelei. Jason whispered, "One... two..."

Before the count of three, Lorelei let out a deafening scream. She crumpled to the floor on her side, writhing as if something were ripping her apart from the inside.

Emmie held Jason back and winced at the woman's distress. There could only be one explanation: Sarah had gotten to Lorelei's spirit. But Emmie refused to let her guard down, and the woman's sickening screech chilled her spine. She had never heard anyone cry out in such pain before.

The spirits that had haunted her only moments before now wavered and veered off in every direction as the cords that connected them disappeared. Flashes of light and heat wildly spun around Emmie, and an intense buzzing sound filled the air as if a thousand flies were swarming a pile of rotting food.

The spirits took turns scrutinizing Emmie and Jason as they freely whipped around the room, peering at them with dazed, tired gazes as if they'd just woken up from a long sleep. Dr.

Albright's spirit swept in front of Emmie, his face now radiating a deep serenity instead of the dull, dead expression she had seen earlier. His eyes sparkled to life and focused in an intense stare. Just as she remembered him.

But the spirits didn't move on. They remained in the room with them, riveting on Lorelei as the woman struggled to stand. They swept through the air but made no motion to stop her.

Lorelei seemed to dismiss the spirits that encircled her, instead standing while hunched forward, her face full of rage. Her naked body revealed a patchwork of burn marks and disfiguration, no doubt the result of her efforts to play with psychic fire.

The woman gazed at Jason then Emmie. "What have you done?" she said in a low moan. "I'll kill all of you."

A cane thumped against the floor beside Emmie. Footsteps shuffled up from behind her and Cecilia stepped into her view. "No, no, no."

Lorelei scowled. "Go back to your room, sister."

"No." Cecilia moved in front of Emmie, dragging her left leg and limping to a stop only a few feet in front of her sister. She bowed her head toward Lorelei as if to submit, but then glanced up sharply. A blazing white light emerged from the young woman's chest.

A spirit formed in front of Cecilia. A radiant white light—an angel of death—but less intense than Lorelei's. The fiery spirit hovered between them as it grew brighter, warming the room in a blinding light.

"Love is patient," Cecilia said.

Lorelei shook her head. "Don't waste your time, sister. Alex is to blame for your troubles. Go back to your room."

"No." Cecilia's body glowed as she limped toward Lorelei. "Ashes to ashes..."

Lorelei scoffed. "Is that all you've got? I trained you better than that, sister. Go back to your room."

"Dust to dust..." Only inches from her sister, Cecilia's angel of death flared in a bright flash and a bolt of energy blasted through Lorelei's chest, cutting the woman's last scream short. The flames ripped through her body, blackening her flesh in a moment.

Even as the flames flashed through her sister, Cecilia leaned in to embrace her. The flames fanned out between them, cutting through Cecilia's body moments later. The young sister let out a pained gasp but didn't scream, and a subtle grin spread over her face before she collapsed on her sibling.

F inn heard Sarah's soft voice and opened his eyes. He was lying face down on the ground with his right cheek pressed against the cold asphalt. A throbbing pain over his whole body pushed him to the edge of fainting again.

Everything came back to him in a flash—that's how it had happened. The heat had swept across his back after he'd thrown himself between Sarah and Lorelei. The excruciating pain stabbed as if someone had thrown a million knives at him. It had gotten much worse despite his brief "rest," and he could have sworn that his back was on fire even now.

But Sarah was kneeling beside him, waving something over his back. It had to be an ice pack. Something wonderfully cool and soothing, whatever it was. The sensation brought some relief as she moved around.

"I'm supposed to do that," Finn said weakly.

"Finn!" She leaned down with a wide smile, almost putting her face against the ground to look into his eyes.

"I'm supposed to save you," he said. "Fat chance, eh?"

"I think you did."

He tried to sit up, but she kept him down. "Don't turn over yet. The burns are extensive."

"How extensive?"

"It's bad."

"Oh... all right, you're the nurse..." He sighed, then turned a few inches so he could see her clearly. She was sitting cross-legged beside him with her downturned palms cupped as she hovered them over his back.

"I thought you were holding a bag of ice over me. That was just your hands?"

She smiled. "Something I learned recently."

"Psychic energy is doing that?"

"You like it?"

"What's there *not* to like?" He closed his eyes for a moment and allowed the cool calmness to soothe him. "The way I go about things in life, that should come in handy."

In addition to Sarah's care, a gentle breeze brushed across his back and bristled his skin from his shoulders down to his thighs. Something didn't feel quite... right.

"Am I naked? Is my butt showing?"

She cringed. "Not exactly... *naked*. Your shirt is burned away, and some of your pants."

Finn winced as a fresh wave of pain swept through him, this one sending him to the verge of fainting again. Within seconds it had passed, but he tensed to prepare for more. "So how many lives have I gone through so far? Buried, frozen, now burned..."

She smiled. At least he could still make her smile.

"You've got a few left but don't push your luck so much." Sarah moved closer and swept her arm under his shoulder. "Now let's get you on your feet."

Finn nodded. It didn't sound like such a big deal until he started to stand up. The pain surged through him again and he let out a guttural moan. The sickening smell of burnt flesh passed through the air, and now he wanted to gag.

"We'll get you to the hospital." Sarah carefully maneuvered around him while bearing the brunt of his weight.

"Aren't you quicker than a hospital?" Finn stood almost straight, but still accepted Sarah's help.

He glanced around suddenly.

"What's wrong?" Sarah asked.

"That was just Lorelei's spirit, right?" he asked. "What about *her*? Is she gone?"

Sarah looked back toward the house. "I feel like she is."

Finn turned to the mausoleum. "And her brother Alex? Do you see his...?"

"Soul? Yes, it's still there."

"Did he have one?"

"Oh yes," Sarah shook her head and sighed. "He did it all for love."

"Love and zombies..." Finn said. "Go together like—"

Suddenly, Sarah held his face and put her lips to his. The moment caught him off guard, and it took him a moment to realize she was kissing him.

In her grasp, his face warmed. "Now I'm burning on all sides," he said.

"You should reward the people who save you, you know."

"Don't mind if I do."

Sarah released him and stepped back. "I think you can walk on your own."

He took a few pained steps and nodded. "Good as new," he lied.

She smiled, seemingly satisfied with his progress, then turned away toward the house.

Love me and leave me? He watched her go, almost forgetting the throbbing pain that extended to even his fingertips.

Maybe it's just as well.

❧ 41 ❧

S arah stepped into Lorelei's bedroom with Finn and spotted Lorelei's aura standing beside two smoldering bodies. Their charred remains lay on top of one another in the same place where Lorelei had sat bathing in light a few days earlier. The nauseating stench made her stomach churn, and she ached, knowing that all three siblings had died on the same day and in the most heart-wrenching ways possible.

A dozen spirits encircled Lorelei, and although Sarah couldn't see them as well as Emmie, she could tell they were standing guard, as if keeping the Temper woman from escaping. Lorelei's aura colors were still a blend of fiery reds and oranges. She was unrepentant even in death.

The spirits of Alex and Cecilia stood to the side, out of the circle, like witnesses ready to present their crimes to an unseen jury.

Emmie and Jason rushed to embrace Sarah as soon as they entered the room, their faces full of exhaustion.

Finn avoided their contact and turned sideways, gesturing to his back while wincing. "I got a little fried too."

"Oh no!" Emmie looked at Finn's backside, then over at Sarah. "Did you call 911?"

"I've got them on speed dial," Finn groaned.

Jason grimaced and shook his head sympathetically. "Oh, man."

"It's all your fault," Finn said quickly.

Sarah touched his arm. "I've been healing him," she told Emmie.

"Healing?" Emmie asked.

"Something I learned recently."

"All right..."

Emmie looked uncertainly at Finn, who nodded and gestured at the room. "So, what's happening? See anything?"

She glanced back at the spirits. Sarah followed Emmie's gaze. "They're all here..." Emmie told Finn.

Jason shrugged. "Can sort of feel them, but can't see anything either."

"Good," Finn said. "I feel less alone. I usually don't get narration at this point."

Emmie and Sarah had already walked over to the edge of the circle of spirits. "I pulled in Alex's spirit," Emmie said.

Sarah nodded and glanced at Alex's wavering form. "His wife and little girl almost came back."

"They died natural deaths, so they could never return." Emmie looked shocked.

"Yeah..." Sarah frowned, remembering the scene. "You don't want to know."

Cecilia's spirit spoke in a soft voice that Sarah heard clearly: "There is an order to things."

Alex's aura shifted in emotion. "I knew, but I still hoped that the door of light would bring them back whole."

"You hoped too much," Sarah said.

"You took advantage of my power," Cecilia told him. "I trusted you; I loved you—but you didn't listen. I tried to tell you so many times, even after I could barely form a word."

"I'm sorry." The darkness swelled around Alex.

Cecilia's aura swept around him in brilliant colors and his aura lightened again. "Brother, love forgives all things."

Alex's aura lightened until it shone, wrapped in his sister's love. "I'm so sorry, Sissy. I love you so much…"

"I forgive you too, Alex," Sarah said. "But it's time to go. I hope you find your family, in light."

Sarah focused on Alex first, releasing him in a warm glow before moving next to Cecilia. Her aura wavered, and Sarah knew she was considering her sister, held prisoner by spirits. Sarah felt Cecilia's regret. Lorelei had loved her, but she had harmed too many others. They had sacrificed the best of the Tempers first, and when Sarah reached out, Cecilia came willingly, and passed with no effort to the other side.

Approaching Lorelei in her prison of spirits, Sarah asked Emmie, "What should we do with her?"

"She's a prisoner of the souls she collected." Emmie gestured to the spirits. "We *could* release her…"

"No," Sarah said sharply. "That would rob them of justice. It seems fitting that she stay here, a prisoner facing her victims until they release her. Let them decide."

Emmie's eyes widened and her mouth dropped open a little, as if she were shocked by this new side of Sarah.

"I'm here, my friend," Sarah said with a tired smile. "It's still me."

Sarah had even surprised herself with her reaction. It wasn't like her to be so tough—but when she turned to look at the darkness that was left of Lorelei, she knew it would take a long time to extinguish those flames and go to a better place.

42

Sarah put the crowning touch on the Christmas tree with Emmie's help: a silver star. Finn had found a dark-haired angel ornament in a box and had suggested that to top the tree, but Emmie had waved it away.

"No more angels!" Emmie said.

Finn looked at it strangely, with a sort of longing for a moment before returning it to the box.

The tree stood in front of the living room window, and they had rushed to make Caine House as festive as possible despite not getting to decorate until Christmas Eve. Plus, they would have to take it all down again in a few days.

Sarah plugged in the lights and stepped back. "Well, I did my best."

Finn and Jason started clapping and whistling from across the room.

Only some scattered ornaments hung on the tree. Just the few that Finn had found in storage, Sarah had taken from her mother and Jason had brought along, but that wasn't the point anyway. They were all together—alive, thank the Hindu gods— and it didn't matter if they had next to nothing to celebrate the holidays, and that no one had gotten time to purchase gifts. None of that mattered at all.

What mattered was that Finn was healing well, and Sarah stepped over to watch him and Jason as they huddled in front of the fireplace. Finn tossed in another piece of wood and the flames crackled louder.

He glanced over his shoulder at Sarah. "Any part of you has the power to light fires?"

"I'll work on that." She smiled, but he looked away. She knew she wasn't to touch him, and not just because of the burns. He had retreated inside himself again, not ready to face big emotions. But she pressed her lips softly together, remembering how his had felt.

"We shouldn't rely on the women for everything." Jason used the fire poker with determination to stir some of the embers beneath the logs in the fireplace.

"I'm about to leave you to it," Finn told him. "Not too happy to be near fire at the moment."

"You're not the first person to come back from Florida with a bad sunburn."

"Yeah, I wish I had earned it on the beach instead of in a weird zoo."

"You had some time on a beach in Cuba," Jason said, just as Sarah was about to walk away.

A pang of jealousy poked at Sarah's heart. Natalia. The thought of Finn spending time on a beach with a woman who was apparently beautiful dampened her spirit a little, but Sarah tossed her head to the side, chasing the thought away. She smiled when Finn countered Jason with a quick, "Blabbermouth champion."

Emmie returned with the punch, and Finn frowned at it as if he would like something stronger, but he accepted it after she used a ladle to pour him a cup.

Jason joined them, filling Sarah's glass before his own, then moved next to Emmie, putting his arm around her waist.

"You know, despite everything that's happened, you have to admire what Dr. Albright and Betty accomplished in their lives," Jason said. "Imagine being constantly on the frontline against people like the Temper family." He pulled Emmie closer. "Your folks did it, too."

"What they were doing deserves respect, I see that now," Emmie said. "It's such a fine line between the use and abuse of psychic energy. An impossible longing blinded Alex to bring his family back. I can't imagine the suffering he went through..."

"And the suffering he caused," Sarah said. "He hurt his sister, but he loved her too. How is any of it right?"

Finn stared pensively at his drink. "That's the eternal struggle, isn't it? Not between good and evil, black and white, but all the gray stuff that gets tossed around in the middle. When we can't tell the difference anymore."

"When we convince ourselves that getting what we want is most important," Emmie said.

"Yes, and that's what the Tempers did," Sarah said. "They had probably followed that dark path for a while, but still clung to the idea that they were special, and their power shouldn't be wasted by thinking like ordinary people. That's what made Lorelei so angry, that by not pursuing their powers and a fight for supremacy against Carey Kali, they were giving up the family legacy."

"She went after revenge. And because of that, the family is gone, legacy and all," Emmie said.

"I haven't loved Carey Kali," Jason said, grabbing a chip from a bowl on the table and popping it in his mouth. "Sort of felt dropped by them ages ago, and since then I've been skirting around them. But they're like the police out there, trying to crack down on people who get too far out of line. I suppose someone has to do it."

Emmie nodded. "But we don't need anyone to school us, or train us, or police us, or manipulate us, okay? We've got a great team here, just us four, and let the other groups do their thing and we'll do ours."

"That's just it," Jason said. "*Will* they leave us alone?"

"Natalia does her thing." Finn seemed to avoid Sarah's gaze. "I got the feeling they leave her alone."

"This isn't the same," Jason said. "Natalia isn't the door of light. Now that Sarah's caught their attention, they'll want to learn more."

Sarah scoffed. "Let them do their worst. I'll kick their asses."

Finn looked up with wide eyes. Jason and Emmie let the silence fill the room. Sarah crossed her arms over her chest as if she'd won a great fight.

As if on cue, a buzzer sounded in the kitchen and she took the opportunity to put on a bright face for them before going to check that the turkey was done.

Emmie followed her. They'd worked for hours to prepare the small meal, and Emmie began putting the other food on serving dishes. "No need to take on the world alone, girl. We're all together now."

Sarah smiled. "We are. The Fearful Foursome."

Only a moment later, as Emmie laid the turkey tray on the counter, Sarah's phone pinged. She wiped her hands and checked the message. "Mom is almost here. No more psychic talk after she arrives."

"Got it. I'll remind Finn and Jason."

Sarah considered the food. "This feels more and more like home, doesn't it?"

"Well, here at Caine's. Or down the street at Betty's. Yes. They're our homes now." Emmie grabbed a mistletoe off the counter and dangled it between them. "Can't forget this. Should I put this on top of your head and Finn's when you're near each other?"

Glancing at the living room, Sarah watched Finn laughing with Jason. She loved that sound. Her face warmed. "You know, Em, I am so sure of everything now."

"You are?" Emmie said with a puzzled expression. "Well, I guess you're... the door of light. Maybe that comes with... certainty?"

"I'm sure he loves me," she said gravely, looking back at Emmie. "And a lot. And I'm sure I love him. It's more than I believed before." She smiled. "But it won't be now. It'll take time —and patience. He's still healing."

Sarah lifted a dish of sweet potatoes from the stove and turned with a mischievous grin. "And if I've learned anything over the last week, it's that love is patient."

GET BOOK 6 IN THE EMMIE ROSE HAUNTED MYSTERY SERIES on the next page!

Read more in the Emmie Rose Haunted Mystery series on Amazon.com!

Raven House: An Emmie Rose Haunted Mystery Book 6

PLUS, get a **FREE** short story at my website!

www.deanrasmussen.com

★★★★★
Please review my book!

If you liked this book and have a moment to spare, I would greatly appreciate a short review on the page where you bought it. Your help in spreading the word is *immensely* appreciated and reviews make a huge difference in helping new readers find my novels.

Shine House: An Emmie Rose Haunted Mystery Book 0
Hanging House: An Emmie Rose Haunted Mystery Book 1
Caine House: An Emmie Rose Haunted Mystery Book 2
Hyde House: An Emmie Rose Haunted Mystery Book 3
Whisper House: An Emmie Rose Haunted Mystery Book 4
Temper House: An Emmie Rose Haunted Mystery Book 5
Raven House: An Emmie Rose Haunted Mystery Book 6

Dreadful Dark Tales of Horror Book 1
Dreadful Dark Tales of Horror Book 2
Dreadful Dark Tales of Horror Book 3
Dreadful Dark Tales of Horror Book 4
Dreadful Dark Tales of Horror Book 5
Dreadful Dark Tales of Horror Book 6
Dreadful Dark Tales of Horror Complete Series

Stone Hill: Shadows Rising (Book 1)
Stone Hill: Phantoms Reborn (Book 2)
Stone Hill: Leviathan Wakes (Book 3)

ABOUT THE AUTHOR

Dean Rasmussen grew up in a small Minnesota town and began writing stories at the age of ten, driven by his fascination with the Star Wars hero's journey. He continued writing short stories and attempted a few novels through his early twenties until he stopped to focus on his computer animation ambitions. He studied English at a Minnesota college during that time.

He learned the art of computer animation and went on to work on twenty feature films, a television show, and a AAA video game as a visual effects artist over thirteen years.

Dean currently teaches animation for visual effects in Orlando, Florida. Inspired by his favorite authors, Stephen King, Ray Bradbury, Richard Matheson and H. P. Lovecraft, Dean began writing novels and short stories again in 2018 to thrill and delight a new generation of horror fans.

ACKNOWLEDGMENTS

Thank you to my wife and family who supported me, and who continue to do so, through many long hours of writing.

Thank you to my friends and relatives, some of whom have passed away, who inspired me and supported my crazy ideas. Thank you for putting up with me!

Thank you to everyone who worked with me to get this book out on time!

Thank you to all my supporters!

Printed in Great Britain
by Amazon